Heartland

From This Day On

by Lauren Brooke

With special thanks to
Elisabeth Faith

ISBN 0-439-65367-3

Heartland series created by Working Partners Ltd, London.

Copyright © 2005 by Working Partners Ltd.
Published by Scholastic Inc. All rights reserved.

12 11 10 9 8 7 6 5 4 3   8 9 10/0
Printed in the U.S.A.   40
First printing, May 2005

Chapter One

❧

"We're going to be late!" Lou exclaimed, glancing at her watch. She turned and shot a nervous look at Amy, who was in the backseat of Nancy's car.

Amy shifted uncomfortably, avoiding her sister's gaze. She knew it was *her* fault that they were rushing to make their dress fittings in town. Amy had been so wrapped up in grooming her pony, Spindleberry, that she had completely forgotten about their appointment. Lou had had to practically drag her away. Now Amy pressed her forehead against the car window, feeling guilty for adding to her sister's stress.

"Don't panic, Lou," Nancy said, slowing down for a red light. "We'll still make it in time."

Lou gave a frustrated sigh. Amy knew what a perfectionist her sister could be. Lou wanted everything to be

1

just right for her wedding. Amy could hardly believe that it was almost November already — and the wedding was only two weeks away!

Amy saw a woman on the street, walking with shopping bags. She paused and looked skyward. Fat drops of rain began to fall, and Nancy flicked on the windshield wipers. The woman raced under the wide awning of the nearest store and began rummaging around in her bags. Amy never saw if she found what she was looking for, because the red light changed and Nancy pulled off again.

"The shop is just one block away. I'll drop you girls off and then park the car," Nancy said lightly, obviously trying to ease the tension in the car. She smiled as she met Amy's eyes in the rearview mirror, and Amy felt a rush of gratitude toward the older woman. Amy and Lou hadn't always gotten along with Grandpa's close friend, but they had all grown much closer in recent months.

Nancy stopped the car in front of a small boutique. A mannequin stood in the window, wearing a spectacular beaded ivory dress with a long train. Lou immediately flung the door open and hurried out of the car. "Thanks for the lift, Nancy!" she called over her shoulder. Then she sprinted inside.

"I guess I'd better catch up with her," Amy said.

"Don't worry. All brides get a little high-strung before

the wedding," Nancy said reassuringly. "Go on in. I'll just find a space and meet you inside."

Amy nodded and slipped out of the car, bending her head against the rain as she ran toward the entrance. The rain on her hair reminded her that she hadn't showered or even combed her hair before leaving Heartland. She was sure she didn't look neat enough for the bridal shop.

As Amy entered, the delicate ring of an unseen bell made a blond saleswoman look up from where she was arranging magazines on a glass-topped table. Lou was nowhere in sight. The woman, who, as Amy vaguely remembered from her last visit, was named Emily, straightened up and smiled. She wore an immaculate cream-colored suit, and her nails were done.

"Hi, Amy. Your sister is in the fitting room, trying on her gown."

"OK," Amy said, feeling messier by the minute.

"Your dress is hanging in the other fitting room," Emily explained, waving toward the back of the store where there was a changing area hidden by heavy gold drapes. "If you need a hand getting it on, just let me know."

Why would I need help? Amy wondered. It was just a dress — all she had to do was pull it over her head, right? She thanked Emily and walked into the fitting room. She pulled the curtain across its rod. As she took off her damp jacket, she caught sight of her reflection in the full-length mirror. It was even worse than she'd thought. Clumps of hay were tangled in her long light-brown hair, and there was a damp patch on her shirt where Spindle had decided to try the taste of cotton. She also had a mark on her face where Spindle had rubbed his mouth against her cheek.

Great, Amy thought ruefully. *Some maid of honor!*

From the next fitting room, Amy heard Lou call out to Emily, "It fits perfectly!"

"Let me see!" Amy chimed in.

"Put on your dress first!" Lou's voice floated back, tinged with excitement.

Amy felt her spirits lift as she reached for her dress. She tugged the lilac silk over her head. As she tried to slip her arms inside the sleeves, her hair fell into her eyes, making it impossible to see the fastening on the dress. She was stuck! "I give up," Amy muttered. "Um, Emily?" she called hesitantly.

Amy heard the curtain rings slide across the rod. Emily gave a light laugh as she stepped into the cubicle and neatly pulled the dress down around Amy's waist. "No worries," Emily assured her. She zipped the dress up with her long, manicured nails. "Happens all the time."

Amy pushed her hair off her face and shrugged her

shoulders a few times to make the bodice sit more comfortably. She looked at herself in the mirror. Her hair was still disheveled, but the pale purple color made her skin look vibrant. Amy slipped her arms into the matching jacket that Emily was holding out for her. The bodice fit snugly, and the skirt fell in soft folds to her ankles. Amy turned this way and that, noticing how the rich fabric's color changed in different lights so sometimes it looked lilac, other times ice-blue. The dress *was* beautiful. She was so used to seeing herself in jeans and old shirts that her reflection in the mirror, in the soft, feminine dress, seemed almost alien to her.

"What are you guys doing in there?" Lou called over the wall. "I'm getting hot in my gown!"

"Hold your horses," Amy replied, smoothing out her skirt.

"Oh, Amy. Is *everything* about horses for you?" Lou teased. "Anyway, I'm not leaving my dressing room until you're ready, too. Otherwise you're going to spoil my grand entrance by coming out after me and tripping on the hem of your dress."

Amy laughed. It was so good to hear Lou being relaxed and silly. "Easy there, diva!" she called back, smiling at Emily.

"Anyway, it's the bride's prerogative to be bossy," Nancy called from outside the fitting room. Amy guessed she had just arrived from parking the car. Emily tugged back the curtain for Amy to walk out. Nancy was sitting on a brocade chair with her car keys still in one hand.

"Thank you, Nancy," Lou said as she pulled back her own curtain. "I plan to exercise that power plenty over the next two weeks."

Amy turned and drew a deep breath. "Oh, Lou, you look . . ." Words failed her as she stared at her sister. Lou was simply dazzling. Her dress was very classic — almost old-fashioned. It was a pale shade of cream and, just like Amy's, came with a fitted jacket. The gown's bodice was form-fitting and lacy, and its long skirt had a slight flare and was slashed down the middle, revealing a white lace underskirt beneath.

"Do you hate it?" Lou asked, suddenly anxious. Her blue eyes widened, and she bit her lower lip.

"Hate it?" Amy cried. "Lou, you're like a bride out of a magazine! It's —"

"Gorgeous," Nancy finished for her. She got up and reached out her hands to both girls. Amy noticed that Nancy's eyes were wet with emotion. She wondered if the older woman was thinking of her daughter, Jennifer, who had died many years ago. "You *both* look gorgeous," Nancy added quietly. "Jack is going to be overcome when he sees the two of you."

Amy squeezed Nancy's hand, then glanced back at Lou.

"Do you think Scott will like it?" asked Lou, smoothing out a wrinkle in the skirt.

Amy heard a note of anxiety in her voice. "Are you kidding? He'll be totally dumbstruck," she told her.

"I hope not so dumbstruck that he can't say 'I do,'" Emily said with a laugh. Lou smiled, but Amy saw that her expression looked strained. Lou wanted so badly for this wedding to be perfect.

"I don't think I've ever seen you in a dress, Amy. You should wear one more often," Nancy commented. "You have a nice figure."

Amy felt her cheeks turn hot. "Dresses aren't exactly practical stable attire," she pointed out. She looked back at Lou, who was piling her hair on top of her head in front of one of the mirrors. Emily walked over to her with a delicate, sparkling tiara.

"Is that what you're going to wear?" Amy asked as Emily helped Lou fix the tiara in her hair.

Lou studied her reflection. "What do you think? Should I weave baby's breath into my hair instead, to match you?"

"No, the tiara's so pretty on you," Amy said. She glanced at Nancy, who nodded encouragingly.

"And you still have time to change your mind," Nancy added.

Emily crouched down to fluff out Lou's petticoat and then stood back. "There's nothing to alter. As long as you don't lose any more weight between now and the wedding, I won't need to see you again," she said.

Lou put her hands on her slender hips. "I'm not planning to," she said. "The only reason I've dropped a few pounds recently is because of all this crazy running around!"

"You wouldn't believe how many brides lose weight right before the wedding," Emily said, her blue eyes dancing. "And how many times they dash back after their final fitting because the dress is loose the day before the big day."

"We can't have that happening," Amy joked. "Last-minute alterations are *not* in Lou's schedule!"

&

After they had arrived back home and carefully carried in the dresses in their plastic garment bags, Amy went out to check on the horses. She opened the barn door and paused. Her boyfriend, Ty, and Joni, the other stable hand, had seen to the horses for the evening, and the sound of hay being quietly munched filled the familiar space. Amy smiled. This was one of her favorite times of the day, when all of the tasks were over and the horses were settled. She made her way down the aisle and stopped at Spindle's stall. "Hey, boy," she murmured over the half door.

Spindleberry had been dozing with his eyes shut,

resting a hind leg. The moment he heard Amy's voice, his eyes opened. He nickered softly and came across to greet her, seeming much less frisky than he'd been earlier that afternoon. Spindle had been at Heartland only since the spring. He had arrived in terrible condition, on his way to an auction house. Brad Baldwin, Ty's father, had been driving the truck and had stopped at Heartland to see if Amy and Ty could do anything to ease the condition of Spindle and the other horses in the trailer. Amy felt a shiver run up her spine at the memory. Three of the horses had died, and the others had just barely made it, thanks to Heartland's vet — and Lou's fiancé — Scott Trewin. He had provided emergency treatment for dehydration and heat exhaustion.

Spindle broke Amy's reverie by thrusting his nose against her hand. She grinned and rubbed his velvety muzzle. "Did you miss me?" she asked. Spindle pushed harder against her hand, hoping to find a treat. "I only came to say good night," Amy explained regretfully. "I can't stay and play."

The colt gave a little sigh and it almost sounded as if he had understood what she was saying. Amy laughed. She loved spending time with Spindle. But she really couldn't stay with him for long tonight. Ty would be coming back in half an hour to pick her up for their double date with her best friend, Soraya, and Soraya's boyfriend, Matt. Amy gave Spindle a final pat and checked on the other horses before hurrying back to the house to get showered and changed. She was really looking forward to the night they had planned. And as fun as the fitting had been, it was a relief to be out of that dress!

❧

Amy was in her bedroom, pulling on a clean pair of jeans, when she heard Ty's horn outside. She glanced out her window and saw headlights sweep around the yard as he turned his car. Amy hurriedly threw on a sweater, pushed her feet into her ankle boots, and grabbed her jacket, pushing her arms through the sleeves as she raced down the stairs. "Bye!" she called to Lou and Jack, who were watching TV in the living room.

Amy let the screen door slam shut behind her and jogged around to the waiting car. "Hi!" she said breath-lessly, opening the door and sliding inside.

"You look nice." Ty smiled, reaching over to kiss her briefly, his finger grazing her cheek. "How did the dress fitting go?"

"Well . . . I'm just glad to be back in jeans." Amy laughed.

Ty grinned and pulled out onto the main road. "I bet you looked great."

"I don't know about that, but Lou sure did," Amy said enthusiastically, and launched into a description of how beautiful her sister had looked in the gown. She rested her hand lightly on Ty's knee as they talked about the wedding and drove along. Amy was just so grateful to have a boyfriend who was as happy for Lou and Scott as she was and didn't seem to mind hearing about endless wedding plans.

The parking lot outside the pizza parlor was almost full, but luckily there was a car pulling out of a space right beside the restaurant's front window. Ty neatly maneuvered into the space, and Amy noticed Soraya and Matt waving at them from a front booth.

"Great, they're already here, and they got a good table," Amy said, waving back as she and Ty got out of the car.

Ty slipped his arm around her and they walked into the crowded restaurant. People were crammed into the comfy booths, chatting and sharing steaming pizza pies. The delicious smell of melted mozzarella and tomato sauce wafted over to Amy.

"Mmm, suddenly, I feel hungry," Amy said as she led the way over to Soraya's booth. She slid into the seat facing Soraya and Matt, and Ty sat beside her.

"Hi, guys. Thanks for joining us!" Soraya greeted them with a broad New Jersey accent.

Amy grinned. Soraya had auditions coming up for drama programs at a few different universities, and she had picked two scenes to perform: one from *Macbeth* and the other from *Cat on a Hot Tin Roof*. She had the idea of doing her rendition of Maggie the Cat in a New Jersey accent, which she hoped would be creative enough to give her an edge over the other auditioning students.

"Guess your rehearsing is going well," said Amy. "That sounded great!"

Soraya wrinkled her nose. "Thanks, but it's not quite there yet."

Matt rolled his eyes. "She does all her scenes perfectly. Believe me, I should know— I hear them a hundred times a day!"

"It's not just about remembering lines. It's about being truly convincing in the character," Soraya insisted. "And you should understand about wanting to really nail something, Mr. Ninety-eighth Percentile. Who retook his SATs last month because he wasn't happy with the excellent score he already had?" Matt grinned as Soraya nudged him in his side. "Are you going to tell them your new score or am I?"

Amy felt her stomach tense. "The results are out?"

"They were posted online today," Matt told her.

"So that means you can look yours up, too," Ty said, glancing at Amy.

Amy hadn't taken her SATs in the spring. She'd been too busy at Heartland and had put off taking them until the previous month. But her scores weren't important to her in the same way they were to Matt, who had his heart set on going to an Ivy League college next year.

She shrugged. "I'll look them up later," she replied. "So, tell us, Matt, what did you get this time?"

Matt spun the menu around on the table. "Fifteen-twenty," he said at last, still looking down. His face was bright red, and he kept his eyes fixed on the spinning piece of paper.

"That's amazing!" Amy exclaimed, feeling a rush of excitement for her friend. He'd worked so hard to get the results and really deserved to do well.

"Congratulations," Ty agreed, reaching across the table to clap Matt's shoulder.

"In that case, it looks like tonight should be a celebratory meal," Amy declared as the waitress appeared at their booth to take their order. They ordered an extra-large pie with mushrooms and peppers, and Cokes for everyone. Then the attention turned back to Matt.

"So are you going to apply early to an Ivy League school?" Ty asked Matt.

Matt nodded. "I hopefully now stand a chance of making it into a decent premed program," he admitted. Then he turned the conversation away from himself. "Aren't you curious about your scores?" he asked Amy.

"Not really," she replied, shrugging off her jacket and draping it over the back of the booth. "I know I want to stay at Heartland next year, anyway. I guess I might do an equine studies program part-time at a local school, but nothing that takes me away from home."

Amy was relieved that the waitress arrived just then with their pizza and sodas. She didn't want her friends to start offering advice about her future. She had thought about it long and hard and had decided that college probably wouldn't benefit her career, because she knew she would be continuing her mom's work at Heartland.

"I've been looking forward to this all day," Soraya announced as she picked up a steaming slice and carefully bit into it.

"You're dribbling." Matt smiled as a drop of tomato sauce landed on Soraya's chin. "Here!" He took a napkin and dabbed at her mouth.

"Why, thank you, Doctor." Soraya laughed. "It's good to see you're already working on your bedside manner!"

Amy thought Matt looked a little uncomfortable at Soraya's teasing, and she wondered why. Matt had wanted to study medicine for as long as she could remember, just like his older brother, Lou's fiancé, Scott.

The rest of the meal passed in a buzz of chatter about Soraya's upcoming audition and the stresses of senior year. Amy realized that, although Ty seemed to be enjoying himself, the conversation had little to do with him. After they had left the restaurant, waved Soraya and Matt off, and climbed into Ty's car, Amy turned in her seat. She looked at Ty's profile, which was softly lit by the lights from the restaurant. "Did you have fun tonight?" she asked him gently. Ty had dropped out of high school, and Amy often wondered if he felt out of place with her school friends, whose lives were so different from his own.

"Sure, I had a great time," he said easily, turning the key in the ignition. "Why?"

"It's just that all we did was talk about school and college and stuff," Amy said apologetically. "And the last thing I wanted was to make you feel left out."

"Hey." Ty turned to face her. "Don't think that. I'm glad to keep up with what Soraya and Matt are doing. They're your closest friends." As Ty smiled warmly at her, Amy felt a rush of relief — and affection.

"There was one thing I couldn't figure out, though," Ty added.

"What?"

"Why *didn't* you look up your SAT scores today?" Ty pressed. "I thought that you'd be curious to know what you got."

Amy stared out the car window into the pizza parlor, where the waitresses were wiping down the empty tables. "My scores aren't that important to me. Matt needs good scores to get into an Ivy League college. Soraya needs decent scores for a drama program, and her auditions mean a lot, too. But I just care about finishing high school and putting all of my energy into working at Heartland."

Ty paused for a moment. "I know all that, Amy. But you're really smart. I don't think you should write off college just like that."

Amy reached over and laced her fingers through his. "Thank you for saying that, Ty. But you know I'd never leave Heartland. Soraya's counting the days until she gets out of this town, but you couldn't pay me to go." Amy glanced playfully at Ty and found his green eyes were still serious.

"Come on, you're not getting rid of me that easily," she said with a laugh, but Ty turned back to the road without a word.

Chapter Two

❧

Amy walked back up from the field, swinging halters from her hand and enjoying the rare burst of late October sunshine on her shoulders. It was Joni's day off, and since Ty was lunging one of their latest arrivals in the schooling ring, Amy had turned the horses out on her own. The horse Ty was lunging, Belle, had been with them only for a few days. The show pony had developed a phobia of being loaded after she had been kicked by a much taller horse in a trailer.

A blue car swept by, heading up the drive toward the house. Amy recognized Scott and Matt's parents, Dr. and Mrs. Trewin, inside. Amy reached the yard just as they were walking up to the front door. Even though it was his day off, Dr. Trewin was dressed in a light-gray suit, and Mrs. Trewin looked equally professional in a dark-blue skirt and matching jacket. Amy was pleased to see that Matt had come with them. He was much more casually dressed in jeans and a sweater.

"Go on in, the door's open," Amy called, waving. "Lou's expecting you." Lou had told her earlier that morning that Scott's parents were coming to talk over last-minute wedding arrangements.

As she hurried to put away the halters, Amy almost tripped over a can of wood stain that was placed just outside the last stall. Amy glanced around for Jack, who had been busy since early that morning painting the stalls, but there was no sign of him. She quickly went around to the barn and hung up the halters before making her way back to the house.

Lou glanced up from setting mugs on a tray when Amy kicked her boots off just inside the door. "Dr. and Mrs. Trewin are in the living room," Lou told Amy as she began pouring milk into the cream pitcher.

"OK. Do you want me to bring anything out?"

"Just the cake," Lou told her, nodding at a coffee cake Nancy had baked that morning.

Amy picked up the cake from the counter and headed into the living room. "Yum!" Matt greeted her, his brown eyes lighting up at the sight of the cake. "I knew there was a good reason for coming over."

"Hands off!" Amy laughed. "After what you put away last night, I'm surprised your stomach isn't on strike."

"That would be impossible." Matt chuckled as Amy set the cake down on the coffee table and joined Matt on the sofa facing his parents.

"How are you, Amy?" asked Mrs. Trewin. "You must be very excited about the wedding."

"I can't wait, even though Lou is driving us all crazy," Amy said teasingly as her sister walked into the room with the tray of coffee.

Lou made a face at Amy. "As my maid of honor *and* sister, I expect you to be a little more supportive!" She laughed.

Dr. Trewin stood up to take the tray from Lou and then made room for her on the sofa. "It *must* be a busy time," he said. "Don't forget that if there's anything you need a hand with, we're just a phone call away."

"I know," Lou said gratefully, pushing a hand through her wavy blond hair. "But I know that you're busy, too." The Trewins were both successful doctors and worked at the hospital on the other side of town.

"It seems we're all leading very full lives at the moment." Mrs. Trewin smoothed her hands over her skirt. "Matt's been so occupied with his college applications. He has to write his essay for Yale today." Amy felt Matt suddenly tense beside her.

Lou cut the cake and began handing it around. "Yale. Wow! Yes, your mom told me about your SAT score, Matt. Congratulations."

"Thanks." Matt gave a lopsided grin as he took the plate from Lou and bit into the cake.

"It was a wonderful result, and one that was well deserved." Mrs. Trewin tucked a strand of brown hair behind her ear and added, "Matt worked hard, and he'll have to keep it up to get through any premed program."

"Mmm." Dr. Trewin nodded in agreement. "But Matt's a natural for premed — and medical school, of course. It's still four years away, but you can never start planning too early."

Matt quickly finished his cake and put his plate on the table with a clatter.

"Do you want another slice?" Lou offered, leaning forward to pick up the knife.

"No, thanks, Lou," said Matt. "Actually, one of the reasons I came over was to see how Spindleberry's doing — I haven't seen him in a while." He glanced at Amy. "Could we visit him?"

"Sure," Amy replied, putting down her own plate and standing up. She felt puzzled. Although Matt always asked how things were going at Heartland, he had never expressed this kind of interest in any of the horses before. Amy wondered if Matt was trying to escape. It suddenly seemed as if he couldn't stand being in the room anymore.

❧

Once they were outside, Matt took a deep breath of the crisp fall air.

"Are you OK?" said Amy.

"What makes you ask that?" Matt fell in beside her as they walked down toward the paddocks.

His tone seemed slightly defensive, so Amy tried to tread carefully. "You just seemed kind of tense back there," she said.

Matt didn't answer, and pushed his hands deep into his jacket pockets. He and Amy walked along in silence.

Then, Amy spotted Spindle. "There he is." She climbed up onto the gate and pointed toward the far corner of the field, where Spindle's dark, leggy form could just be made out. He was grazing beside two other horses, Liberty and Bear, that had arrived with him on the auctioneer's truck.

Amy let out a long whistle and called Spindle's name. The gelding raised his head and looked in their direction.

"Over here!" Amy called, fishing in her pocket for a horse cookie.

Spindle stared at them a while longer before moving slowly away from the other horses. With a sideways toss of his head, he broke into a beautiful, fluid trot.

"He's looking great," Matt commented as he climbed

the gate to sit beside Amy. "I can't believe how much taller he is."

"Yeah, and he's really filling out. It's scary how fast he's growing up," Amy said, feeling a rush of pride as Spindle came to a halt beside them. "Here." She broke the cookie in two and gave half to Matt. She held out her own piece for Spindle to lip off her hand, then gestured to Matt that he should do the same. Matt stretched out his hand, and Spindle snorted heavily before taking the cookie.

"Have you started riding him yet?" Matt asked as Spindle noisily crunched on the treat.

"No, it's still too soon for that. But I've spent lots of time brushing him and getting him used to having a bit in his mouth. He's doing really well," Amy said enthusiastically. "Soon we can start thinking about lunging him." She glanced at Matt and saw that he was gazing off into the distance. *He's not listening to a word I'm saying,* she realized. "We have him booked for his first circus act next week," she continued. "His specialty is balancing on one leg while juggling three balls."

"Hmm," Matt said distractedly. Then he frowned. "Wait, *what* did you just say?"

"Oh, nothing." Amy tried not to laugh. It was all too obvious that Matt's mind was elsewhere. "Is everything OK?" she asked, hoping he would open up this time.

Matt sighed and picked at a splinter on the top bar.

Spindle also let out a deep breath when he realized that there were no more cookies. The colt turned away and began to walk back to the other horses, his tail swishing.

Watching him go, Matt said at last, "I guess all this talk about the future is kind of bugging me."

"Really?" Amy was surprised. Matt had always been so confident about where he was heading after high school. He was the last person she expected to feel uncertain about what lay ahead.

Matt nodded. "Lately, I've just been feeling all this pressure. Like my parents are making all the decisions for me. They've always expected that I'd follow them into medicine, and I've kind of just gone along with that. But now . . ."

"I guess it's normal to feel anxious before college," Amy said. "But you're such a good student!"

Matt flicked a splinter of wood onto the ground. "It's not that. It's just that I need to know that going premed is the right thing for me — not just the right thing for my parents."

Amy struggled to find the right words. "Does anyone else know you're feeling this way?"

"No. I basically just made sense of what's been bugging me for the last few weeks," Matt confessed. "I don't want to bring up the subject with my parents until I've decided what I'm going to do. Normally, I would tell Soraya, but I don't want to distract her from her auditions.

Anyway, it's not like we're getting to spend a lot of quality time together now. She's pretty wrapped up in rehearsing." He hesitated, as if he were afraid of saying too much. "I'm glad I told you, though. It sort of helps just talking about it, you know?"

Amy squeezed her friend's arm. "I wish I could be more helpful," she said. "It's hard for me to relate, because I feel pretty secure about my plans after high school." She took a deep breath and looked directly at Matt. "All I can say is that I think your parents will support you in whatever decision you make. They want you to be happy, and they're probably so focused on premed because they think that's what *you* want, too. There's still time to change your mind."

"I guess you're right," Matt said.

"Just promise me one thing," Amy said teasingly. "Promise you won't do anything crazy — like run off to the circus with Spindle, OK?"

Matt's face split into a broad grin. "I promise," he said. "I'm not going into any act with a horse that can juggle more balls than I can!"

❧

Amy sat deeper in the saddle and urged Sundance to lengthen his stride. "C'mon, boy!" she called. Sundance's ear flicked back at the sound of her voice, and he obediently put on an extra spurt of speed. Amy grinned as

Sundance carried her away from Ty and Joni, who were cantering along the ridge at a slower pace on Liberty and Bear.

Sundance, Amy's beloved buckskin, was fitter than the rescued horses, and Amy was able to keep him cantering for a while before she sensed he was tiring. Slowing him down to a balanced trot and then a walk, she reined him to a halt at the highest point of the ridge. Without the noise of Sundance's hooves on the track, there was utter silence, broken only by the call of a bird somewhere over the distant treetops. A pumpkin-colored leaf spiraled down through the air in front of Amy, like a tiny propeller. She reached out her hand to catch it, admiring the bright splash of color against her black riding glove.

Sundance turned his head and nickered as Bear and Liberty walked up the tree-lined path toward them. Amy felt a surge of pleasure at how healthy the two horses looked. It was hard to believe that, only a couple of months ago, they were hovering between life and death in the cramped trailer. Amy saw Joni lean over to rub Liberty's neck as the pretty gray mare picked her way along the track, and Ty patted Bear's chestnut shoulder. Amy smiled. That was one of the things that she loved most about Heartland — they were such a strong team, all equally passionate about their work with troubled horses. Amy felt a small thrill shoot through her at the thought that soon she would be able to work full-time as part of that team. As soon as she graduated, she'd be able to commit herself even more fully to everything at Heartland.

Amy's excitement must have shown on her face, because when Ty halted beside her, he remarked, "You're beaming."

"Am I?" Amy laughed. "I guess I'm just loving getting to ride on a day like this." She swept her hand at the view that stretched out for miles, vibrant with the gold, crimson, and pumpkin colors of the trees. The country-side looked as if it had been scattered with small, bright jewels.

"It's fabulous," Joni agreed. "Autumn is my favorite time of year."

Amy nodded. "Too bad Soraya can't be here," she said, thinking how Saturday had always been their day for riding out together. It seemed like ages since Soraya had come over to Heartland, now that every spare moment was taken up with rehearsals. Amy hadn't even had lunch with her at school that past week.

Ty glanced at his watch. "We should head back. The farrier's coming in half an hour."

Reluctantly, Amy shortened Sundance's reins and turned him to face down the path. But she couldn't feel too disappointed. *After all,* she thought, *it's not long until I'll be able to ride out every day.* She thought back to her earlier conversation with Matt and just wished that he could feel the same confidence about his future that she felt about hers.

❧

In school on Wednesday, Amy's American history teacher gave them a research project that was due in one week. Amy decided to get started on it right away, since she knew that the more time passed, the closer they would be to the wedding and the less time she would have for schoolwork. After dinner that evening, she ensconced herself in Lou's office to do some research online.

While she was waiting for the page to load, Amy sipped her coffee and glanced around the room. Normally, Lou's desk was buried under mountains of files and papers that were needed to run the business side of Heartland. Amy was surprised at how neat the desk was now — practically clear. She realized that her sister must have been working even harder than usual to take care of everything before she and Scott took off for their honeymoon.

Amy looked back at the screen. She set down her mug on a coaster with a picture of a beautiful Thoroughbred on it. A thought struck her. Since she was online, she figured she might as well look up her SAT results. *Why not?* she thought. Amy typed in the address, then logged on to the site. She filled out her personal information, and then drummed her fingers on the desk as the page slowly loaded. Then she scrolled down and came to her score.

Amy gasped. That couldn't be right. She narrowed her eyes at the screen. There was her verbal score, and then her math score, and then the final calculation, staring back at her in bold black type: 1310.

Disbelieving, Amy shook her head. She hadn't dreamed she'd break twelve hundred, let alone thirteen. True, she'd studied hard in the weeks before the test, taking practice exams in the Kaplan workbook she'd borrowed from the library. Her grades in school weren't stellar, and Grandpa sometimes chided her about that. She'd wanted to prove to him that she could work hard and at least pull off a decent score on her SATs.

But *this*!

Amy's heartbeat sped up as the implications of her score sank in. She double-checked that her personal information was correct — to make sure that the score didn't belong to some other Amy Fleming — but it was indeed the one who lived on Forest Ridge Drive in Virginia.

Amy pushed her chair away from the desk and began searching the opposite bookshelf for the thick paperback college guide Lou had purchased for her ages ago but that she'd never even looked at. When Amy came upon the book, she cracked open the stiff spine and turned to the entry for the local community college, where Amy had considered taking equine studies courses the following year. The college listed its minimum SAT score requirement — and Amy's score was way over their average.

Amy sat back down in the chair and, her fingers trembling, flicked through the book until she found the entry for Virginia Tech, the state university located in Blacksburg. Amy knew that the school had an excellent preveterinary program. Amy ran her finger down the page, and when she read the application requirements, her blood roared in her ears. Her score fit their requirements as well. And even though her grade-point average wasn't great, she saw that it also made the minimum requirement.

Meaning that, if she wanted to, Amy could probably get into Virginia Tech. The possibilities unfurled in her mind: leaving home to live on the Virginia Tech campus, where she would study to become a veterinarian. A real four-year college experience, followed by graduate work. She'd never even considered it before.

Suddenly, Amy felt dizzy. It was all too much. She needed to get out of the office and try to clear her head. She went to the barn and found her footsteps leading her instinctively to Sundance's stall. The gelding nickered as Amy slid her arms around his warm golden neck and rested her head against his mane. Being close to Sundance made her feel somewhat steadier. She took a few deep breaths to calm her racing pulse.

"Oh, Sundance, what should I do?" she whispered.

She was annoyed that the thought of Virginia Tech had even come into her head. Now that the thought was there, she couldn't shake it free. Ty's words from the other night echoed in her mind: *I don't think you should write off college just like that.* But how could she even consider leaving Heartland when she felt so safe and secure just standing with Sundance now? And working with Ty on a daily basis. She didn't need to pursue becoming a vet. Her whole career was already mapped out for her, right at home.

Amy felt as if she were being pulled in two different directions. She had been so sure that her future meant staying at Heartland. But now a different future was revealing itself, and she couldn't see how she could decide between the two.

Chapter Three

❧

Amy pushed a forkful of pasta into her mouth but didn't really taste the thick cheese sauce. Her mind had been miles away all morning. She hadn't told a soul about her SAT scores — not Lou, not Grandpa, not Ty, and not even Matt and Soraya, whom she was meeting for lunch.

"Are you trying to tell us something?"

Amy was jolted out of her thoughts by Matt's deep voice. She looked up to see him and Soraya standing by her table. She blinked a few times, wondering if he had somehow read her mind.

Matt nodded his head at Amy's books, which were piled on the chair beside her. "If we didn't know better, we'd think you didn't want any company today," he joked.

"Sorry," said Amy, feeling flustered. She reached out

to scoop the books off the chair, glad that her long hair was hiding her red cheeks.

Matt sat down in the seat Amy had cleared, and Soraya dropped into the chair facing them. There were dark circles under her eyes and she was frowning. Amy suddenly remembered that Soraya had an audition that afternoon. She gave her friend a sympathetic smile. "Nervous?"

"A little." Soraya pushed her tray away. "I can't eat this."

"You should try to eat something. You need the strength," Matt urged. Amy couldn't help thinking that he sounded like a concerned doctor, and she gave him a small smile.

"I can't fit in any food with all those butterflies in my stomach," Soraya moaned. She glanced up at Amy and made a face. "Some actress I'm going to be if I get stage fright this bad."

"You'll do great," Amy told her, reaching out her hand and squeezing Soraya's shoulder.

"If I remember my lines." Soraya gave a nervous laugh.

"Do you want to practice now?" Matt asked. "We'll listen."

Amy nodded encouragingly. Soraya cleared her throat and focused on the wall behind Amy's head. She launched into her monologue with a perfect English accent, sounding as if every one of Shakespeare's words were her own.

Amy couldn't help feeling drawn completely in. Soraya's rehearsing had certainly paid off. But as she neared the end of her speech, Soraya hesitated. She blinked a few times and her words faltered to a stop. She looked horrified. "I forgot my next line! I knew I would!"

"You remember." Matt reached out and caught her hand. *"Nor heaven peep through the blanket of the dark . . ."* he began. Amy was impressed by his dedication to Soraya — he'd learned her lines as well!

Soraya's shoulders sagged. "Maybe *you* should be trying out for this instead of me, Matt. Don't you ever get tired of being good at everything?" She smiled weakly, and pushed back her chair from the table. "I have to go now. My mom's picking me up early."

Matt stood up. "Call me as soon as you're done, OK?"

"Me, too," Amy said. "I'll be thinking about you."

Soraya nodded. "Thanks, guys. See you later."

Matt watched her leave the crowded cafeteria and sat in the seat she'd just vacated, opposite Amy. "Why do I feel like I've just messed up?" he asked Amy.

"Oh, you know Soraya. She's just temperamental like that," Amy said. "All great actresses are."

Matt gave her a rueful smile as he pulled his tray across the table and bit into his sandwich. Amy picked up her fork but still didn't dig into her pasta.

"Did you buy that just to play with?" Matt teased as she poked listlessly at the penne.

Amy glanced up at his amused expression. "I don't really want it," she admitted.

"Is there something I should know about the food today?" Matt asked, looking pointedly at Soraya's untouched tray.

"I've just got stuff on my mind," Amy admitted. "School stuff."

"Did you look up your SAT scores?" Matt asked. When Amy nodded without looking up, Matt asked carefully, "Were they pretty low?"

"I kind of wish they had been," Amy said. She sighed, looked up, and told Matt her score.

"Wow," said Matt. He blinked a few times, then grinned at her. "That's awesome, Amy."

Amy didn't respond right away. Matt stared at her for a moment. "Wait, why did you say you wish you'd scored lower? That's crazy."

"Isn't it?" Amy laughed. Suddenly, all her pent-up emotions tumbled out. "It's just that, up until I saw that score, my future seemed so clear to me. I hadn't ever thought seriously about college. But now . . . I feel like it would be a waste not to at least . . ." She trailed off.

"You definitely have a lot more options open to you now," Matt said finally.

Amy chewed her bottom lip. "I know," she said. "I feel like I can't handle even thinking about changing my plans. I was really looking forward to being full-time at Heartland."

Matt folded his arms across his chest. "Just because you go to college doesn't mean that you won't end up at Heartland," he said thoughtfully. "You could always study something that you could use to complement your work there."

Amy's thoughts immediately went to the preveterinary program at Virginia Tech.

"But," Matt went on, "if you do decide to go to college, you should decide pretty soon. Maybe you should make an appointment with your guidance counselor." He leaned forward. "And I'm here for you if you need to talk about anything."

Amy felt a rush of relief. Since she had started seeing Ty, and Matt had begun dating Soraya, they had drifted apart, and she suddenly realized how much she had missed their friendship. "Thanks, Matt," she said. "That means a lot to me."

He smiled at her, his brown eyes warm and kind, and Amy knew he felt just as grateful for their talk at Heartland.

For the rest of the week, Amy told no one else about her SAT scores. She figured the others assumed that she didn't care enough to look them up. Of everyone, Amy thought Lou would have been more curious about her SAT results if her wedding hadn't been one week away.

For once, Amy felt a guilty jolt of relief that her sister was too distracted to remember.

❧

On Saturday morning, Amy was busy raking fall leaves into a pile at the edge of the driveway, while Joni and Ty were turning the horses out. Amy was getting a start on sprucing up the garden in preparation for Lou's wedding. She had already finished the yard and was concentrating on the path in front of the house. In seven days' time, Lou would walk down that path in her cream gown, before making her way around to the side lawn where the tent would be.

"Feel like some hot chocolate?"

Amy looked up to see her grandfather watching her efforts from the front door. "That would be great," she said thankfully. The sweeping was keeping her warm, but her face was pink from the cold late October air. There had been an unexpected drop in temperature over the last couple of days, and although it wasn't as cold as winter, it was still a shock at this time of year.

"Is Lou back from town yet?" she called as Jack began to close the front door. Lou had gone into a panic over the cold snap and had made a last-minute appointment with her dressmaker for capes lined with fake fur, to go over the dresses.

"She just called to say she's on her way back. She's

afraid she won't be in time to meet the delivery truck and asked if you'd take care of it."

Amy frowned. "What delivery?" she started to ask, but Jack had gone inside. She shrugged and began filling the wheelbarrow with the mountain of leaves she had raked together. Her back twinged when she straightened up, and she was glad to abandon the task when Jack called her into the kitchen a while later.

"You're back." Amy smiled at the sight of Lou standing by the sink with her hands cupped around a mug. She was surprised she hadn't heard Lou's car on the driveway, but, then again, she had been very intent on her raking.

"I got here just as Grandpa took the kettle off the stove," Lou told her, glancing at Jack, who was running a cloth over the kitchen counter.

"Perfect timing," Amy said, and pulled out a chair to sit down at the table. "Ooh," she groaned, pressing her hand into the small of her back.

"Are you OK?" Lou asked, concerned.

Amy grimaced. "Those leaves are a killer."

Lou threw her a grateful look. "Thank you so much for taking care of them."

Amy noticed that her sister's cheeks were flushed a bright shade of pink, as if she hadn't stopped running since getting out of bed that morning. She wished Lou would slow down before she totally wore herself out. "So, did you get the capes?" Amy asked.

Lou nodded. "They already had all of our measure-
ments, so it's not going to be a problem to make capes to
match our dresses." Her shoulders sagged. "But there's
still so much to do."

"Maybe you should order scarves and hats to match,"
Jack teased, joining them at the table. "Winter may
be two months off, but you can't be too careful!" He
chuckled.

Amy sipped her hot cocoa. She wasn't sure the capes
would be necessary, either — she thought they'd both
be sweaty messes with all the work Lou still wanted
them to do. Amy doubted the day of the wedding would
be any different.

"You think I'm stressing, don't you?" said Lou, her
forehead creasing with worry.

Jack reached out a thumb to smooth away the frown.
"I think that if you don't take it easy on yourself, you're
in danger of being too tired to enjoy your wedding. I just
want the day to be perfect for you, hon."

Amy nodded. "I agree with Grandpa," she said
between sips. "Things are coming together. We all know
what we need to do. And Dad and Helena will be here to
help soon, too."

Lou's eyes shone brightly as she looked from Jack to
Amy. "Thanks, guys. You don't know how much your
support means." She gave a smile before sniffing and
reaching for a tissue. A vehicle could clearly be heard

pulling up outside in the yard. "That must be the delivery truck," Lou said, checking her watch as she pushed back her chair. "They called earlier and said they'd be here before four."

Amy saw that her sister had instantly transformed back into her efficient, organized self. "Hang on," she called after Lou who was already heading out the door. "I'll give you a hand." Amy glanced at Jack, who shook his head in exasperated sympathy, and then she hurried after her sister.

❧

Out in the driveway, a white delivery truck was parked close to the house, its rear doors open. A tall man in dark-blue overalls stood next to Lou, grasping a large ceramic pot that held a perfectly manicured tree.

"Isn't it just lovely?" Lou enthused to Amy. She reached out a hand to touch the globe of glossy dark-green leaves on an impossibly slender trunk. "There's another one still in the truck. They're a gift from Scott's coworkers. How about you put it next to the door?" Lou suggested, returning her attention to the man supporting the plant. "Amy, don't you think it will look nice with one on each side of the door?"

Amy was about to reply when the truck's side door unlatched and a red-haired boy with a small frame jumped out of the truck. The boy met Amy's gaze with a broad grin, and she couldn't help but smile back at the freckle-faced youngster.

"Evan, zip up your coat," called the man. He bent over to set the tree down and then rushed over to Evan's side just as the boy began to tug at the zipper on his blue ski jacket. Once the zipper was tight under Evan's chin, the man looked at Lou. "Where did you say you wanted these?" he asked, heading back to pick up the pot he had set down.

"I'll show you," Lou offered.

Amy stifled a laugh when, after they were left alone, Evan began sizing up the second plant. He folded his arms and ran his eyes up and down the length of the tree. Amy could tell he was wondering if he could carry the pot, but she was sure it would be too heavy for him. Not wanting to know how Lou would react if something happened to the tree or its lovely green china pot, Amy decided it was best to distract Evan. "Hey, do you want to look around the yard for a few minutes?" she offered. "We could go see some horses."

The boy's sharp blue eyes darted across to the barn and then back at Amy. "All right. I'll just ask Chris." He broke into a run after the man Amy had assumed was his father. He sprinted around the corner of the farmhouse just as quickly. "I can, but I have to put my hat and scarf on first." He sighed, trudging around to the front of the truck.

Amy bit her lip to disguise her grin as Evan reappeared swathed in a huge red scarf and matching hat. The youngster glanced suspiciously up at her. Amy looked away and started to walk toward the barn. "This row of stables is empty right now," she said over her shoulder, walking past the stable block, which smelled fresh and clean from the new layer of paint. "Right now, all the horses are stabled in the barn." She pushed open one of the double doors and stood back to let Evan go in.

Amy then walked ahead of him, so she could lead the way down the center aisle. She soon realized that only her own footsteps were sounding against the concrete floor. Amy turned around to find that Evan had stopped in front of a bench that was pushed up against a stall. He was holding something up to his face. "What's this?" he asked, lifting a small glass bottle so that Amy could see.

"That's lavender oil," she said, realizing that she had left it out that morning. "We use it to treat some of the horses."

"It smells good."

"Yeah," Amy said, taking the bottle out of his hand and unscrewing the cap.

"We sometimes use it to massage their faces and necks," she explained. She held the bottle out so he could take a good whiff. "The smell is supposed to help horses relax."

"That makes sense," he responded with a shrug. "If it works for people, why not horses, too?"

Amy let out a light laugh as the boy headed down the aisle, glancing into the stalls. "Well, you're very open-minded for your age."

"How old do you think I am?" he queried without turning around.

Amy winced. She never liked that kind of guessing game. Looking at Evan's height and slight frame, she thought that he might be in second or third grade. "I don't know," she said. "Maybe eight?"

"What?" Evan's face squinted in a scowl. "I'm almost ten," he declared.

"Sorry," Amy quickly apologized. She was about to explain that Evan must be small for his age but then thought better of it. Instead, she began to describe some of the other remedies they used to treat the horses.

Evan seemed to move past his indignation and listened to Amy's explanation. "I bet the horses trust you," he commented.

Again, Amy was struck by the boy's composure.

"Do you know a lot about horses?" Amy asked.

Evan looked down and scuffed his toe on the floor. "A little," he said. "I've got a pony."

"You do?" Amy asked, feeling surprised that he hadn't mentioned it before. "What breed is it?"

Evan shrugged his thin shoulders. "It's just a regular pony," he said, and then walked off down the aisle, peering over the doors of the other stalls. "You don't have that many horses here," he said as Liberty poked her head over her door with her ears pricked forward.

"Most of them are out in the fields. We turn them out in the morning and bring them in at night," Amy said as she walked across to join him. "We kept Liberty in this morning so I can do some training work with her."

"Why?" Evan asked as Amy leaned over the stall door and scratched the gray mare's forehead. Libby let out a deep breath and lowered her head until it was resting on Amy's shoulder.

"We rescued her a while ago and now we're working with her so she can go to a new home. We think she'd make a great pleasure horse," Amy explained. "We want to find new owners who will really appreciate her," she told Evan, who was gently running his hand along the mare's satiny neck.

"Was she sick when you got her?" Evan asked, not taking his eyes off Liberty's gentle eyes.

"I'm afraid she was. For a while, we thought we might lose her," Amy replied, and began to describe how the rescued horses had all been suffering from heat exhaustion when they arrived.

"Did you think you'd have to put her down?"

Evan asked the question in such a flat tone that Amy blinked. She wasn't exactly comfortable talking about those details, especially with someone so young. She swallowed slowly. "Well, we did have to put one of the horses down," she admitted. Sadness welled up inside her as she pictured the palomino mare that had been too sick and dehydrated to save. "But we never give up on an animal easily. We do everything we can until there's absolutely no chance at all of saving them."

Liberty lifted her head off Amy's shoulder and wandered across the stall to pull at her hay net.

"Chris and Janet put down their sheepdog last week," Evan said, looking Amy straight in the eyes as if he were challenging her to defend what had happened. "They said Rusty was real old."

"Chris and Janet?" Amy questioned, curious as to how they were related to Evan. She knew Chris was the guy in the delivery truck.

"They're my foster parents," Evan explained.

"Well, I'm sure that they would only have put him to sleep if it was absolutely necessary," Amy said, feeling unnerved by the conversation. "Was Rusty sick?"

Evan nodded.

"If he was so sick he couldn't get better, then they might have wanted to stop his suffering," Amy offered awkwardly. "He might have been in a lot of pain." Just then, the clatter of hooves on concrete distracted Evan. Ty appeared at the top of the aisle, leading Bear. Ty raised his eyebrows at the sight of Evan draped over the door of Liberty's stall.

"Ty, this is Evan. His dad is delivering some trees for the wedding," Amy said.

"Foster dad," Evan corrected. He walked up to Bear and held out his hand for the chestnut to sniff. Bear's muzzle hovered over Evan's flattened palm, searching for a treat. "Can I lead him into his stall?" Evan asked. He didn't seem at all bothered by the fact that the gelding towered over him.

"Of course." Ty flashed Amy a bemused smile as Evan reached for the braided leather reins. "His stall is the next one down on the right."

Evan patted Bear gently on his shoulder before tugging at the reins to lead him forward. "Did you ride him?" he asked as he led Bear into his stall.

"I lunged him for a while, and then I took him out on the trails," Ty answered, rubbing the back of his neck. "He went really well," he told Amy. "He's getting better every time I take him out. He's so laid-back. His new owners are going to be thrilled. He'd be a great first horse."

"Why can't he stay here?" Evan interrupted. His voice was muffled as he stuck his head under the saddle flap to undo Bear's girth.

Ty shook his head at Amy and then went into the stall to take the saddle from Evan. He slung it over the partition wall before explaining to Evan Heartland's practice of finding new homes for the rescued horses so they would have the room to take on other horses that needed their help. Ty slid the bolt on Bear's stall into place after Evan stepped out.

"Do you have any other horses in here?" Evan asked next, standing on tiptoe to look over Bear's door.

Amy was amazed by how comfortable Evan was with them. "Belle is in the last stall at the end of the row," she told him. "She's here to get over her fear of trailers. She's very sweet. Do you want to see her?"

Evan nodded and started down the aisle. "Thanks for your help," Ty called, winking at Amy as he gathered Bear's tack in his arms.

Amy hurried to catch up with Evan, who had already reached the end stall and was peering inside. "She's pretty small," Evan commented, holding out his hand for the mare to sniff.

"You're right. She's only thirteen-two hands. But we don't need to ride her. We just have to get her to trust us enough to go into a trailer," Amy replied, stretching her hand out to ruffle the pony's forelock.

"You can do it," Evan said with great confidence, scratching Belle's nose. Amy smiled at him appreciatively but did not get a chance to respond.

"Evan!" The call echoed through the barn.

"That's Chris," Evan explained quickly. "I guess he's ready to go," he said, frowning a little.

Amy found herself wishing she had time to take the boy around the paddocks and the other Heartland highlights, but she appreciated that Chris must be on a tight schedule. "Come on. I'll go with you," she told him.

"Bye, Evan," Ty called as they passed Bear's stall.

"How many horses are here when it's full?" Evan asked Amy as they walked out of the barn.

"Well, we have stalls for twelve, but in the summer there's room for more if some stay in the paddocks at night," Amy told him. "It's good that things are quiet right now because my sister is getting married soon, so we're busy getting ready for her wedding," she explained as they walked toward the house in the cool, damp air.

Chris was standing alongside the truck. "Evan, your scarf's undone." He reached out to tuck it into Evan's coat.

Evan frowned and pulled away. "I'm fine," he muttered.

"We were inside the barn, so it was warmer there," Amy offered, trying to ease the tension.

"Have you thanked the young lady for showing you around?" Chris prompted, straightening up and nodding at Amy.

"It was no problem," Amy said hurriedly. "We had fun. Evan's welcome anytime."

Evan turned around and shot her a brief smile before clambering into the truck and pulling the door shut.

Amy suspected he was embarrassed by his foster dad's overprotective concern. But Chris seemed nice. He smiled his thanks at Amy again and slid into the driver's seat. Amy waved as the engine started and clouds of smoke billowed from the exhaust. The truck reversed and headed down the drive.

Chris pulled over to the right to let another vehicle pass, and Amy immediately recognized Scott's Jeep. She walked across the gravel path to greet him as he parked and climbed out. Scott clapped his hands and rubbed them together with a grin at Amy. "How are you, Amy? Are you coming in?" He nodded his head at the house. "Is Lou inside?" he immediately added, not giving Amy a chance to answer his previous questions.

Amy's first thought was that Scott might have had one cup of coffee too many. She tried to figure out what could be bothering him, but she couldn't think of anything but the wedding — and he had been a relaxed groom up to that point. "I don't know where she is, I've been out in the barn," Amy said. All at once she thought of one thing that might make him excited like this — her SATs. After all, Scott was practically part of her family now. *What if Matt told Scott about my score? What if Scott's going to announce it to Lou or Grandpa?* she thought frantically as she hurried after Scott, desperate to stall him. But he was already standing beside Lou when Amy burst into the kitchen, and by the look on his face, he was about to broadcast his news. Amy held her breath, her heart hammering as Scott looked around, his eyes bright. "Guess what I just found out?" he began, before swinging Lou around by her waist.

"Scott! Stop it!" Lou scolded breathlessly. "I've got a knife in my hand!" She retreated to the kitchen counter next to Jack, who had stopped rinsing vegetables in the sink. Amy licked her dry lips, more convinced than ever that Scott was about to let on that he knew her SAT results. Obviously, he'd assume that Lou and Jack knew, too. Amy had no idea how she would explain why she had told Matt her results but not shared them with her family.

"I've been offered a new job!" Scott exclaimed, and Amy felt her shoulders slump with relief. Scott looked at Lou. "I still can't believe it. I'd be a partner in a big practice, so it'd be a big raise, and the chance to gain a lot of experience."

"What? How, when, where?" Lou held her hands up in the air as if trying to slow Scott down.

"Well, it would mean a bit of an upheaval, because it's kind of soon and it's out of state. We'd have to relocate to California for a couple of years, but I tell you, Lou, it would be an amazing opportunity for us." Scott nodded to emphasize his words.

Amy crossed to the table and sat down on a chair. After a brief moment of relief, her heart had started thudding again. The fear that Scott had been about to announce her SAT scores was nothing compared with the shock of this news. She glanced at her sister, who stood with her back to the kitchen counter, the paring knife still dangling loosely in her hand. Under other circumstances, their grandpa's expression would have been comical. He stood with his mouth slightly open as the freshly washed green pepper dripped water on the floor. But it was Lou whom Amy was most concerned about. Her sister's face had drained of color and her eyes were riveted on Scott. She squinted slightly as if she didn't understand what he was saying.

"California?" she asked eventually. Her voice rose in alarm. "You're really prepared for us to move all the way across the country? This is my home, Scott. What were you thinking?"

Chapter Four

At first Scott looked deflated, but then he took a deep breath and lifted his chin. "I know this is *your* home, Lou. But we aren't going to live at Heartland. We aren't going to live with my parents, either," he pointed out, with a forced laugh. "We're going to have our own home, and it can be wherever we want it to be."

Lou walked a few steps toward him. "Exactly," she said. "Wherever *we* want."

Scott pushed his hand through his hair. "Is that why you aren't willing to be happy for me? Because I didn't ask your permission before I got the job offer?"

"My *permission*?" Lou's voice shot up an octave. "You know it's not about that. I am happy that you're excited about this position. But *I* can't get excited about you

51

taking a job in California and just following you there. That doesn't sound like a joint venture to me. This is supposed to be a partnership."

A deep frown creased Scott's brow. "I don't get it. I've just got a really great job offer. And *they* approached me. That's a big deal in my field. I thought you'd at least be proud of me."

Lou crossed her arms. "Well, I am proud of you for that, but I'm surprised that you think I'm willing to give up my work at Heartland without a thought. My work here is important to me."

Amy noticed Jack quietly wiping his hands on a dish towel before heading for the living room door. As awkward as Amy felt, she couldn't figure out how to leave. It was clear that this was something for Scott and Lou to sort out on their own, yet Amy felt personally invested. This was her sister! But then Grandpa shut the living room door, which was almost always left open, behind him when he left. Amy knew she had to give Lou and Scott space, too.

With a last glance at her sister's defiant expression, Amy pulled open the kitchen door. She saw Ty leading Belle across the yard and watched as he raised his hand to wave at Joni, who was steering a wheelbarrow toward the muck pile. Amy figured it was perfect timing. If she hurried, she could slip into the barn for Sundance's tack. She didn't want to see anyone right now. She just needed to tack up Sundance and ride out on the trails to sort through her jumbled emotions.

✖

A couple of weeks earlier, Amy, Joni, and Ty had spent a few hours building a set of fences along a path that branched off from the main riding trail. The jumps were simple, made of brushwood and fallen timber. Amy remembered that they hadn't had the opportunity to try out the new trail, so she decided it would be a great way to chase Lou and Scott's argument from her mind. As she rode up Teak's Hill, she let Sundance trot on the more level stretches to loosen his muscles. When they reached the entrance to the path, she tightened the left rein and felt Sundance set his jaw and stiffen his neck. He was used to staying on the main track.

"It's OK, I know what I'm doing," Amy told him, patting his neck. "Just trust me. You're going to like this." Sundance's ears flicked back, and this time when she squeezed her right leg against him, he moved obediently off the main trail. The moment Sundance's hooves hit the soft turf of the narrow trail, Amy shortened her reins and pushed him into a canter. The trail widened around the next bend where the first of the jumps lay waiting. Amy crouched down against Sundance's neck to avoid a low branch and had to steady her pony as he tried to lengthen his stride.

"OK, now!" she whispered as they rounded the bend. A few yards ahead, there was a tree trunk that had fallen across the track, which had seemed like the perfect start to their cross-country course. Sundance snorted and gave an eager bounce as Amy pointed him at the jump. She steadied him and then pushed him forward, all her worries about Lou and Scott vanishing from her mind as she concentrated solely on the thrill of riding the trail.

The next jump was a stream that Sundance cleared easily, giving a half buck as he landed. "Good boy!" Amy shouted as he cantered along the path, the breeze whipping back his mane. Although the cold air bit against Amy's face, she didn't care. They cantered some way before the first of the homemade jumps came into sight. Joni and Ty had found a makeshift picket fence that had surrounded an old, broken-down shack. They separated it into two sections and moved them across the trail to make an easy in-and-out obstacle. Sundance popped over the first jump and put in three even strides before gathering himself for the second.

Amy slowed him, knowing that the path dipped down immediately on the far side of the fence, but she felt a surge of adrenaline as Sundance pulled against her and skidded downward, struggling to find his balance as he headed for a wide ditch at the bottom of the hill. Just in time, he launched over the pit, and Amy leaned her weight forward to help as he boldly clambered up the next bank. She could hear pebbles bouncing down the bank as his hooves dug into the sandy hill.

With a snort, Sundance heaved himself onto level land, with which the original trail connected.

"Good boy!" Amy exclaimed, patting the pony's damp neck. "You were great," she told him. The buckskin gelding snorted again and swished his tail. Amy tilted forward and wrapped her arms around his neck as Sundance energetically strode ahead. But as they began to head down the trail toward home, the thrill of the ride started to ebb as Amy's thoughts returned to Lou and Scott's argument and all the possible repercussions.

Amy absentmindedly twirled Sundance's mane in her fingers. She had just gotten used to the idea of Lou getting married and moving away from Heartland — but moving out of Virginia! Amy couldn't bear the thought of not having her sister around, and she didn't know how they would manage without her. If Lou did leave, it would be even more important that Amy choose to work at the stable full-time.

Amy's uncertainty brought on a wave of longing for her mother. Amy believed Marion would have had sound advice for both Lou and Amy regarding the future. There were so many decisions to make, and time kept moving on. Amy rode along with only the sound of Sundance's hooves against the trail as she struggled to work out what path Marion would endorse, but all that came into her mind was a fleeting image of her mother's gentle smile.

As Sundance instinctively turned down the fork that led back to the barn, Amy saw Joni leading Spindle up from the field. It occurred to her that the stable girl would be spending far more time with the young horse if Amy decided to go away to college. She had found it hard enough to leave Spindle behind for a few days when she visited her friend Carey at Ten Beeches during summer vacation. She felt a surge of jealousy as she considered someone else taking Spindle through the various stages of a young horse's training.

Amy's gaze was still focused on Joni and Spindle when Ty passed in front of them. Amy's heart plunged. She had successfully avoided thinking about what her pursuing a veterinary career would mean for her relationship with Ty. Even though he had promised to support her regardless of her decision, Amy knew why she had not yet told him about her scores. She wasn't ready to deal with the idea of not seeing him every day. She also wasn't ready to see the possible disappointment in his eyes. Her decision was already hard enough.

Just then, Joni looked up at Amy and waved. Amy felt another twinge of envy at the happy, relaxed way the stable girl began to walk toward her. Joni had made it clear when she applied for Ben's job that she wasn't considering college at this point. She was determined to prove to her parents that she was committed to a career working with horses. Amy had always assumed that she would do exactly the same thing — it was one of the reasons why she had felt so at ease with Joni — but now she was standing at her own crossroads, and she wasn't sure whom she had the most in common with anymore.

"Nice ride?" Joni asked, halting Spindle a few feet away. The young gelding stretched out his nose to greet Sundance with a friendly nicker.

"Yeah, we went on the new jumping trail," Amy offered, trying to keep her voice light. "It was great. How's Spindle?"

"A perfect gentleman, as always," Joni replied.

Amy was ready for Sundance's predictable bad-tempered reaction, and the moment his ears flickered back she reined him back a few paces. "Be nice," she said sternly as she kicked her feet free of the stirrups and jumped to the ground. Sundance rubbed his head against her arm, and Amy guessed that he was feeling sticky under his bridle from the workout. "I'd better get him inside. He's anxious for a rubdown," she told Joni. "He's a demanding customer."

"I'm glad you liked the trail," Joni continued, walking Spindle a length behind Sundance. "I was going to see if you and Ty wanted to try it out this afternoon, but I got sidetracked."

Amy halted Sundance and tapped his shoulder as he

began to paw at the ground. "Sidetracked?" She looked back at the stable hand.

"I noticed that there was half a gallon of that specially treated paint left after Jack had finished the stalls," Joni explained. "So I thought I'd give the front gates a fresh coat — especially since the guests will be driving through them next week. I also finished applying creosote to the walls to preserve the wood."

Amy felt a shot of guilt. How could she be at all resentful when Joni was so generous? Ever since Joni had taken over Ben's position, she had been nothing but cheerful and hardworking. "Thanks, Joni, that goes far beyond your job description," she said sincerely. "Maybe we can all go for a ride tomorrow."

"That would be great." Joni smiled as Sundance began pawing the ground again.

"I'd better take him in. He's the last pony I want to hold a grudge against me." Amy quickly ran up the stirrups, then took the reins over Sundance's head and clicked softly to him. With a swish of his tail, the gelding walked in beside her, with Spindle and Joni following close behind.

❧

Amy didn't sleep very well that night. She had so many things running through her mind that she kept waking up with a start, thinking she had overslept. It was a relief when she finally glanced at her alarm clock and saw that it was early morning. She shivered as she swung her feet out of bed and decided to take a hot drink down to the stables when she went. She pulled on a thick sweater and jeans before treading softly down the stairs, not wishing to disturb Lou or Jack. When she pushed open the kitchen door, she was surprised to hear the familiar gurgle of the coffeepot ending its brew. Jack had his back to her as he reached into a cupboard for a mug.

"Is there enough for two, Grandpa?" Amy yawned.

"What are you doing up at this hour?" Jack asked.

"I couldn't sleep," Amy replied, curling up in the soft chair in the corner of the room.

"Me neither," Jack admitted. He poured coffee and a splash of milk into the two mugs before crossing the room and handing one to Amy.

"Thanks, Grandpa," she said gratefully, closing her hands around the hot china. The house was still chilly since the heating had only just come on.

Jack pulled a chair from the table and turned it to face her. As he sat down, Amy asked him, "Has Lou said anything else to you about moving to California?"

Jack let out a deep breath before answering. "When Scott left yesterday, he told Lou that he hadn't accepted the job yet, but that he'd need to give them his answer soon."

"So Lou does get a say in this, then," Amy murmured, taking a sip of the hot coffee.

Jack frowned. "To be fair, Amy, I don't think Scott ever intended to make a decision without talking to Lou first. I think he was excited, and he wasn't careful enough when he told her about the job. Lou was very quick to accuse him of not thinking." Jack gave another big sigh. "We know Lou will look out for herself, don't we?"

Amy didn't say anything. She didn't feel like being charitable toward Scott right now. She glanced up at Jack. "Do you think that they'll end up going?"

Her grandfather hesitated for a long time before replying, "I really don't know, honey. But if worse comes to worst, then Scott says it's only for a couple of years. It could be really good for him. It's good to see someone young so dedicated to his job."

Focusing on the mug in her hands, Amy thought ahead to two years' time. It seemed so far away. She would be almost twenty. And she had no idea what her life would be like then. Would she be continuing her mom's work at Heartland, or would she have left to follow a completely different career path? And if she chose to become a vet, would she someday be tempted to leave her family in order to get a better position somewhere else?

In the silence that followed, Amy concentrated on the sound of the clock ticking on the mantelpiece, but she suddenly became aware of a noise from just outside the window. It sounded like something rustling in the bushes, and Amy froze. She glanced at Jack and saw him looking equally alarmed. Had one of the horses gotten loose? Or was it something else?

Grandpa set his mug on the table, and together they went to the window overlooking the yard. Jack pulled back the curtain and leaned close to the glass. It was still dark outside, and although Amy strained her eyes, she couldn't see a thing.

"I'll put the outside light on," Jack said, making his way to the back door. When he flicked the switch, the yard was flooded with harsh yellow light, and Amy let out a gasp. Just outside, nosing at one of the plants in the window box and blinking his eyes against the sudden glare, was a sturdy pony that Amy had never seen before.

Chapter Five

❧

"There's a horse outside!" Amy called to Jack in amazement, but her grandpa had already disappeared. Amy quickly pulled her coat and scarf off the peg and shoved her feet into her boots before running after him.

The pony was wearing a thickly lined horse blanket and a matching blue halter, which Jack gently took hold of. The buckskin gelding snuffled at Jack's hands in a friendly way. "He seems fine," Jack told Amy as she came up to join them. "But he's done a number on the mums."

Amy gave the uprooted flowers in the window box a glance, wincing at the thought of Lou's reaction, before reaching her hand toward the pony. The pony pricked his ears forward and pushed his nose against Amy's shoulder. She ran her hand down his neck and noted that it was warm and slightly damp. "He's really warm," Amy observed out loud. "He must have come a long way."

She could see the pony's sides moving in and out underneath his blanket as if he were out of breath. "I wonder if he got out of his paddock somehow," she mused. "I don't recognize him. I don't think I've seen him in anyone's field."

Jack thoughtfully stroked his jaw, his fingers making a rasping sound against his unshaven skin. "You could be right."

"Well, he's quiet enough," Amy commented. Now that she was closer, she could see that the pony had a dappled coat. "He's very pretty," she added, tickling the whiskered area on the pony's chin. "And someone's taking good care of him, if his blanket is anything to go by."

Jack nodded. "Why don't you put him in the barn?" he suggested. "He shouldn't be out in the cold if he's sweaty. We can make some phone calls later on to see who he belongs to."

Amy took hold of the gelding's halter and led the pony toward the barn. Her bare feet were loose in her boots as she gingerly sought out the familiar path in the dark. The first stall on the right was empty, so Amy slid back the bolt and led the pony straight in. "I'll get you something to eat," she promised as she shut the door. The pony nickered as if in response.

When Amy walked back into the barn carrying a hay net, she was greeted by a chorus of whinnies from the other Heartland residents. Sundance's golden head shot over his door, his ears pricked forward. A moment later, Jasmine's pretty black head appeared over the adjoining stall.

"Hey!" Amy called out sternly as Sundance flattened his ears and bared his teeth at the mare. When Amy went into the first stall instead of coming to him, Sundance kicked his door, making it rattle against the bolt. "OK, OK," she called. "You want your breakfast, I get the message!" She tied the net through the ring on the back wall and patted the mystery pony briefly on the neck before hurrying out to get a start on the morning feeds.

After such an early start, Amy had already collected and rinsed out all of the buckets before Ty and Joni were due to arrive. She stacked the last pile along the feed room wall and glanced at her watch. She had just enough time to give Spindle a short visit before getting ready for school.

Spindleberry was dozing with his eyes shut, and Amy stood watching him for a few moments. A voice in her head reminded her that, if she went to Virginia Tech or any other four-year college, she wouldn't be able to share early morning visits with Spindle or Sundance.

And that was just the beginning. Amy leaned her head on her arms on top of the partition wall and thought, for what seemed like the millionth time, of everything she would miss if she left Heartland. Somehow, there was no real consolation in thinking that she could always come back during vacations and then when her schooling was complete. Even the thought of six weeks away was enough to make Amy feel depressed, never mind several years. Life at Heartland was forever changing and moving on, and she wanted to be a part of that — not just a visitor.

With a rustle of straw, Spindle stamped his front leg and then opened his long-lashed eyes to stare at her. "As for you, you would be approaching middle age by the time I finished vet school," Amy said softly.

A door banged, making Spindle throw up his head in surprise. Muffled voices drifted into the barn from the feed room, and Amy guessed that Joni and Ty must have both arrived at the same time. She left Spindle to go and tell them about the mysterious early morning arrival of their newest visitor.

🐍

"He just showed up by the house?" Ty asked, narrowing his green eyes.

Amy nodded. "And he didn't come with any clues — other than a snazzy blanket and a taste for window boxes."

"That must have been freaky, waking up to that." Joni grinned, pulling off her scarf.

Amy pushed a strand of hair out of her eyes. "Actually, I was already awake," she admitted. "I didn't get much sleep last night."

Ty glanced at her with a concerned expression. "Are you OK?"

Amy smiled and shook her head, knowing she should not have given Ty a cause for concern. "I'm fine. I've just got a lot on my mind. I'll tell you about it later," she added, looking down at her watch. She had a meeting with the guidance counselor that morning and she didn't want to miss it. "I think Grandpa's going to make some calls to try and find out where the pony's from, but can you keep an eye on him to check that he's OK? He seemed pretty happy when I left him."

"Of course we will," Joni said. She flapped her hands in the air at Amy, shooing her away. "Now go, or you'll be late!"

❧

Amy showered and changed with her usual lightning speed, and as she walked into the kitchen and glanced at the wall clock, she was pleased to see that she had enough time to sit down and have breakfast for a change. "Morning," she said to Lou who was already at the kitchen table, leafing through a pile of mail, while Jack poured coffee into a long line of mugs.

"How much coffee are you planning on drinking, Grandpa?" Amy asked with a grin.

"Very funny," Jack replied. "Actually, I invited Joni and Ty in; I thought they'd appreciate a coffee with the cold wind that's blowing." At the same moment, the door opened and Ty walked in.

"Hey. Joni will be here in a minute. She just wanted to check on the new pony first," Ty said, taking a mug from Jack and blowing on the hot coffee.

"Ah, yes, our mysterious visitor." Lou looked up from her mail. "Do you have any idea where he might have come from, Amy?"

"None at all. I figure he must have gotten loose and somehow found his way here," Amy said, pulling out a chair and sitting across from Lou. "His owner is bound to miss him this morning and contact the police, so hopefully we'll track them down before too long."

She broke off as the kitchen door burst open and Joni hurried into the kitchen. Her face was pale. "You'd better come quick," she gasped. "There's something wrong with that pony!"

❧

Amy's stomach dropped as she hurried across to the

door and yanked on her boots before racing across the yard, just behind Joni. The group skidded into the barn, the commotion unsettling the horses, who snorted uneasily. The moment she set eyes on the pony standing in the far corner of his stall, her mouth went dry. The buckskin gelding was standing with his head hung low; his sides were heaving in and out, and he was fighting for every breath with a terrible rasping sound. As soon as Ty took in the scene, he tugged open the stall door.

"What's wrong with him?" Amy asked, hurrying across the straw and running her hand across the gelding's wet neck.

Ty shook his head, his mouth set in a tight line. "I've never seen anything like this. It happened so suddenly." He looked up at Joni, who was hovering in the entrance to the stall. "Do you have any ideas?"

"No." Joni's face was pale. "I'll call Scott," she told them, spinning on her heel before rushing past Jack.

Amy's grandfather joined them in the stall. "Lift his head up for me."

Amy and Ty grasped either side of the pony's halter and tried to lift his head. Ty wedged his shoulder under the pony's jaw, forcing him to hold his head up. Jack first examined the buckskin's nostrils, then put his ear to the pony's chest. As Jack stood up, the pony thrust his neck out and coughed, a great hollow wheezing cough that made his body tremble.

Jack shook his head. "We need to get him out of here. We don't know what kind of infectious disease he might have, and we have the other horses to think of."

Amy's heart began to pound. It was bad enough to see the pony in distress, but to think that the other horses might catch the same illness was horrific! She would never forget the trauma when a virus had swept through Heartland and they lost several horses at once. She rubbed the pony on the nose and felt her mouth go dry again. He seemed to be getting warmer by the minute, and a gauzy film was gathering on his eyes. "I'm sorry, boy, but we have to move you," she said. "Come on." She clicked her tongue and tugged gently at the halter. The pony stood listlessly, stretching out his neck to avoid taking a step. Amy gave him another tug, and when he shuddered, she was certain he would collapse.

Jack reached over the pony's withers, and Ty positioned himself by his hindquarters. "C'mon, boy," Ty urged as everyone encouraged the pony forward.

Painfully slowly, the pony dragged his hooves toward the door. "Steady," Jack muttered as he stumbled out of the stall. Ty and Jack stayed on either side of the horse to help maintain his balance. Amy glanced back at Ty and saw her own fear reflected in his eyes. There was nothing worse than seeing an animal suffer without knowing how to help. She hoped Joni was able to get through to Scott.

They halted the pony several feet from the barn. A thick, creamy discharge was leaking from his nostrils. His breath rose in the air like billows of smoke, and Amy worried that the icy temperature might be making him worse. As the pony's body shuddered with a deep, throaty cough, Amy wondered if he just had a bad cold, but it was far worse than anything she'd seen before. And she had never known a cold to take hold so quickly. Amy reached up to rub the gelding's ears, massaging them gently. The pony stood quietly, hanging his head, but he seemed to take some comfort in Amy's attention as he leaned his forehead against her chest.

The kitchen door snapped open and Joni jogged across to them. "Scott will be here in a couple of minutes," she blurted out. "I got him on his cell phone. He said he was already on his way over here to see Lou."

The news filled Amy with temporary relief, but she knew there were things they could do for the pony in the meantime. His neck was lathered, and every breath was an effort for him.

"I'll go get a bucket and sponge," Ty offered.

"Do you need me to do anything, sweetheart?" Jack asked.

Amy concentrated for a moment on murmuring softly to the distressed pony and rubbing the base of his ears in small circles. Underneath the blanket, the pony's flank was still heaving. She glanced up at Jack. "Can you get the bottle of lavender oil? It's on a shelf just inside the barn. It's all I can think of to try to calm him down."

Jack headed off to get the bottle of oil. When he returned, he handed it to Amy, breathing hard. Amy unscrewed the top and tipped a few drops onto her fingers. Then she began to rub the liquid into the skin around the pony's eyes. The gelding stood quietly for her, but his breaths were sporadic and shallow.

"So, what's wrong with this guy?" Scott's voice made Amy jump. She had been so focused on the sick pony, she hadn't even heard his Jeep pull up.

"He's a bit of a mystery," Jack told him. "He just turned up in the yard early this morning, and he seemed fine then."

"We put him in the barn, and when Joni checked on him later, he was like this," Amy added, watching Scott pull his stethoscope out of his bag. Joni joined them from the barn and helped Amy strip back the pony's blanket. The group fell silent with concern as Scott pressed the metal disc against the pony's flank.

Ty arrived with a bucket and sponge as Scott was finishing his examination. He set the bucket down and waited while Scott told them all to take a few steps back. Scott then placed his thumb and index finger on either side of the pony's larynx and gave a careful pinch. Almost immediately, the gelding pitched his body forward and let out a deep, hollow cough. As his body convulsed a second time, a sticky gob of phlegm hit the cold ground.

Scott nodded.

"Oh, gosh," Joni said.

"Do you know what's wrong?" Amy asked, searching Scott's face for a sign of how serious the illness might be. She went over to hold the pony's head, running her hand down his nose repeatedly.

"I think he's got COPD," said Scott.

"COPD?" Ty echoed, moving to stand next to Amy and giving her arm a quick squeeze. "Is it contagious?"

"Chronic Obstructive Pulmonary Disorder is its full name," Scott explained. "It's usually triggered by an allergic reaction. Like to the dust from hay or bedding."

"Can we cure him?" Amy asked, her voice high with anxiety.

Scott shook his head. "You can't cure him of the disorder, but we can do things to keep it under control. It's actually fairly common, kind of like asthma in humans. Some cases are more severe than others." He pointed to a defined muscle that ran along the gelding's side. "Do you see that faint line along his flank? That's a strain mark. This pony has been coughing a great deal over a long period of time."

"So what can we do?" said Amy desperately.

"I'll give you some medicine to put in his feed twice a

day. Since his symptoms increased when you put him in the barn, it could be that he's allergic to hay and straw," Scott said. "That's common with COPD. I suggest you keep the blanket on him and turn him out in the paddock until you find his owner."

Amy reached up to brush the pony's forelock out of one large, dark eye. She then ran her finger lightly down his face. Even with Scott's instructions, she still felt bewildered. "Thanks, Scott," she whispered. "I've never seen anything like it before. I just didn't know what to do."

"None of us did," Jack added.

"It can be really frightening if you don't know what it is," Scott agreed. "The reaction can be very extreme. But he's already looking better than when I arrived. That reinforces the probability that he was reacting to the hay and straw in the barn."

"Well, if the crisis is over, then I'm going back into the house to make myself presentable," Jack said, rubbing his hand over his face. "I still haven't shaved this morning, and Nancy's coming over soon." Amy managed a smile as Jack winked at her and turned toward the house. Watching him go, she realized she had something she should be doing as well, but she couldn't leave until she knew Scott's plan for treatment.

Scott handed her a white container with a screw lid. "Put two scoops of this into a small bucket of coarse feed before you turn him out. You'll need to put it into his food twice a day until all the powder has been used up. It should clear up his cough."

Amy took the plastic container and looked at Scott. "Is there anything else?" she asked.

"No, that should be it for now." Scott gave her a professional nod and then leaned over to zip up his medical bag.

Amy glanced at Joni. "Can you watch him, please? I need to get going or I'm going to be late. Just take care of the powder in the feed, and I think maybe we could give him some Mimulus, too. It will ease his shock from not being able to breathe. And," she hesitated, feeling utterly torn, "can you look through my mom's book to see if there's anything she suggests for COPD?" It was the first time that Amy had handed her mother's precious notes to Joni to use. "Ty can help you if you need anything." Amy glanced up to give Ty a smile of gratitude and saw the baffled expression on his face.

"You're going to school now?" Ty had a note of surprise in his voice. Amy suspected why. Usually, when a crisis occurred at Heartland, Amy would persuade Lou to let her stay home. But she knew her appointment with the guidance counselor might be the chance to figure out the consuming question of what she was going to do next. For the first time ever, Amy knew that school would have to take priority.

"The worst is over," Scott said before Amy could find a response to Ty. He picked up his bag and glanced at Amy. "I'm heading inside. I think Lou and I have some things to talk about. And a coffee would be nice."

"Thanks, Scott." Amy smiled. She remembered Scott's initial reason for coming to Heartland that morning. He and Lou had to talk about the job offer. Amy felt a rush of gratitude, knowing that Scott had been willing to put the displaced pony first, even though he probably was eager to make up with Lou. She gave the pony's nose one final rub before leaving him with Ty and Joni. Then she hurried back to the house, a few steps behind Scott. Quickening her pace, she reached the kitchen door just before he did and reached up to grab her schoolbag off the hook. "Thanks, and good luck," she said as she raced past him once again and tore down the drive, praying that the school bus would be late as usual so she would make her appointment in spite of the morning's drama.

Chapter Six

❧

Amy sat on the chair outside the guidance counselor's office, absentmindedly twirling a strand of hair around her finger. She knew that she ought to be planning the questions she wanted to ask, but she couldn't tear her thoughts away from the sick pony. If Scott hadn't been on his way to Heartland, who knows what would have happened? *One day, having a vet based at Heartland could make the difference between saving a horse's life and losing it,* she thought just as the office door opened with a faint click.

Ms. Noble, the guidance counselor, looked down at her and smiled. "Hi, Amy. Would you like to come in?"

Amy picked up her bag and followed the tall, red-haired counselor into the office. "Take a seat." Ms. Noble walked around to the other side of the desk and waved her hand toward the chair facing her. "Would you like a glass of water?"

Amy shook her head. "I'm OK, thanks."

Ms. Noble leaned her elbows on her desk and pressed her fingers together to make a steeple. "So, what can I do for you today? It's been a long time since we last talked, hasn't it?"

Amy hesitated. Amy had met Ms. Noble only once, when she was a freshman. Every first-year student was required to talk with a guidance counselor to discuss class selection and postgraduation expectations. Amy couldn't even remember how that meeting had gone. Now, more than three years later, Amy wasn't sure she had any more of a clue. She was almost afraid to start talking. What if she set off a chain of events that changed everything?

The phone on the desk rang, and Ms. Noble apologized to Amy as she picked up the receiver. Amy didn't mind; it gave her a chance to think about what she wanted to say. She shut out Ms. Noble's voice and looked around the room, thinking how neatly organized it was, unlike the other school offices where she had been that tended to have books and files stacked on every available surface. Ms. Noble even had small porcelain bowls in a neat row next to her in-box, filled with sharpened pencils, Post-its, and paper clips. Amy was supposed to meet with Ms. Noble after her mother's death, but Amy had convinced Lou and Grandpa that it would be easier to transition back to school without touchy-feely time with the administrative faculty.

"Right." Ms. Noble cut into Amy's thoughts as she replaced the receiver. "Where were we?" Amy blinked a few times, trying to focus. "I have your SAT scores," Ms. Noble prompted, opening a thin blue file and glancing down at the sheet of paper on top. "They're very impressive. Your parents must have been thrilled."

Amy swallowed hard as Ms. Noble quickly corrected herself, "Your family, I mean."

"I haven't told them yet," Amy admitted, watching Ms. Noble's thinly penciled eyebrows raise into perfect arches. "I guess I'm not sure what I want to do yet, and I didn't want to tell them . . ."

"In case they pressured you," Ms. Noble finished for her. She placed her fingertips together again and rested her chin against them. "Don't worry, you're not the first person to feel like that."

Amy nodded. "Not that they would try to pressure me," she said quickly. "But they might think college is the obvious choice for me, and I need to make that decision for myself, so that I know whatever I choose, it's for the right reasons." She stopped and took a deep breath. She hadn't been meaning to say all that.

"It sounds as if you've been doing a lot of thinking," Ms. Noble said encouragingly. She pulled a pen and pad toward her and jotted down an Internet address. "This is an excellent site for links to all of the accredited, four-year colleges," she said. "I think you're making a wise decision."

Amy blinked. "But I haven't made any decision yet. I mean . . ." She faltered.

Ms. Noble glanced up. "I thought you wanted to talk to me about your college options."

"Sort of," Amy said. "It's just that I had everything planned out for after graduation, and all of this has been a big shock."

Ms. Noble sat back in her chair. "What had you planned to do?"

"Continue working at Heartland," Amy said, the words sounding comfortable and familiar. "It's all I've ever thought about doing. But then, I never thought I'd do well on the SATs. I've never really put much effort into my grades." She smiled ruefully at the counselor.

Ms. Noble touched one hand to her upswept auburn hair. "I've looked at your records, and I agree that over-all they're not . . . stellar." The corner of her mouth lifted in a smile. "But it's nothing you can't overcome this year with a lot of hard work. You've proved that you're more than capable with your SAT score, and you'd get great recommendations. Your dedication to your family business hasn't gone unnoticed by your teachers — in fact, I'd say that it's something that will definitely be in your favor in your applications to colleges. If you decide that's the route that you want to take, of course."

Amy found herself warming to the counselor. It seemed like she was genuinely confident that Amy could make up her own mind about this. "I've been thinking about all of the extra work that I'd have to do, and I know that I can do it," she said slowly.

"Well, then, let's look at some colleges to give you an idea of what options you have and what the application requirements are." Ms. Noble pushed back her chair and went over to a bookshelf.

"I've already got an idea of what college I want to apply to," Amy said, resting her forearms on the desk and rolling a pencil back and forth.

Ms. Noble paused with her hand in the air. "You do?"

Amy nodded. "Virginia Tech has a program that I'm interested in."

Ms. Noble returned to the desk and sat down again. She raised her eyebrows to encourage Amy to go on.

"They have a prevet program, and I think my scores are good enough to get me in." Amy felt as if every word was taking her away from the people and horses and situations she knew best, but she kept going. "I know it will mean a lot of work this year, and even then there are no guarantees that I'll get in. I never really thought about college until I saw how it could help at Heartland. Then it made more sense." Amy took a deep breath. "I guess I just needed to talk it through with you to see what you thought before I mention it to my family."

Ms. Noble ran her tongue along her upper lip as she flipped through Amy's file. "If you are really willing to do the work to get your class grades up, then you have a strong chance of being accepted."

"I guess getting accepted is the first step," Amy said, "but getting through the four-year program is even more intense."

"Everything you've said makes sense to me. I understand you still have some thinking to do, but it sounds like you have the dedication to succeed no matter what you choose to do," Ms. Noble said, glancing at the wall clock. "You know I'm here anytime you want to discuss things. However, if you don't mind my saying," Ms. Noble said, then paused dramatically, "I think your next step should be telling your family about your SAT score. You're going to need their support if you do decide to apply for college."

Amy smiled sheepishly. "Thanks for seeing me," she said as she stood up.

"That's what I'm here for." Ms. Noble smiled. "I know making your decision won't be easy, but I'm confident that you'll do what's best for you and Heartland in the long run."

Amy bit her lip thoughtfully as she left the office, the counselor's final words ringing in her ears.

❧

Lou had arranged to pick up Amy after school. As Amy walked down the steps outside the building, wrapping her scarf around her neck, she could see that her sister had managed to find a space right next to the sidewalk. "Hi," Amy said, pulling open the passenger door and welcoming the blast of warm air from the car heaters. "How's the pony doing? Did you track down his owner?" The mystery gelding had been on her mind all day.

Lou looked up from the bridal magazine she had been flipping through. "We didn't have any luck, but the police said they were sure they'd get a call once he was missed. He was doing fine when I left. Joni's been visiting him every half an hour, judging from the number of times I've seen her cross the yard."

"Oh, good." Amy felt the tension she had stored up drain away. Getting the pony healthy again was even more important than finding his owner, which they could concentrate on now that they knew he was going to be OK.

"Here, take this," Lou said, handing Amy the dog-eared magazine. "I don't know why I'm even looking in there. We don't have time to do anything else with the flowers, but I can't help but gaze at the perfect centerpieces and bouquets. It's an addiction!" She threw her hands up.

Amy stifled a laugh. "So, I guess the wedding's back on?"

"Oh, come on, Amy," Lou chided. "You know it was never in jeopardy. Scott and I just needed some time to consider each other's perspectives. To tell you the truth, it was a good thing," Lou said in a confessional tone. "I'm glad we tackled that now, so we know each other's priorities."

"And?" Amy prompted. Lou rested her hands on the steering wheel and stared out the windshield.

"And it's important to me to stay close to home at least until after you graduate," Lou stated slowly, flashing Amy a teary smile. "I'd like to stick around longer, but we'll see. For now, Scott promised he'd turn down the job in California."

"Fantastic!" Amy exclaimed.

"So you're stuck with me!" Lou reached across to affectionately yank on Amy's hair.

Amy returned the friendly gesture. Then, stretching her seat belt to its full length, she reached over and gave her sister a hug. "I don't know what we'd do without you," she said with her face pressed against Lou's shoulder.

Lou hugged Amy back and then pulled away. Happiness radiated from her as she started the car. "Scott said that he hadn't really thought about how important my job at Heartland is. When he saw my reaction to his announcement, he was suddenly hit by how much I've put into Heartland. It would be hard for me to leave everything that I've helped to build. I'm really invested in Heartland. I hope we never have to go far away."

Lou's words instantly left a painful, hollow feeling in Amy's stomach. Little did Lou know that she was facing a similar dilemma. Amy feared that if she didn't confess everything now, she might never be able to confront Lou and Jack. She had a difficult decision to make, and she knew she couldn't do it alone. She took a deep breath. "Well, since we're sharing, I've got some good news of my own."

"Really?" Lou said, flicking on the turn signal and pulling out.

Amy glanced at her sister's profile as she concentrated on negotiating her way onto the congested road. "I found out my SAT score," she said. "I got a thirteen-ten."

"Amy! That's great!" Lou exclaimed. "I'm proud of you. Now we've got a scholar running Heartland." She reached over and squeezed Amy's arm, without taking her eyes off the road. "This calls for a celebration! But with the wedding on Saturday, I'm not sure we can fit it all in."

Amy felt a bit taken aback. One of the reasons she had been reluctant to tell Lou was because she had thought her sister would insist on her going to college with a score like that. But it looked like it hadn't even occurred to Lou that Amy might want to put her SAT score to some use. It was true that Amy had agreed to take the standardized test only because Grandpa had been nagging her, but Amy had assumed Lou would see things differently now — like Amy did.

Lou continued chatting about the checklist of details left to organize before the wedding, but Amy let her voice wash over her. She was discouraged that it seemed as if this was one decision she was going to have to make on her own.

✑

Lou parked the car in front of the house, and Ty came out to help unload the groceries. "Isn't it great news about Amy's SATs?" Lou beamed, juggling four shopping bags while trying to shut the car door with her hip.

"What?" Ty frowned and looked at Amy.

Amy looked blankly from Lou to Ty. The SAT discussion in the car had been over for at least fifteen minutes. Lou had had so little to say at the time that Amy was confused why she would use it as a conversation starter now — and why she would think it was her place to publicize the news. Looking at Ty's dazed face, Amy knew she shouldn't have let him hear about the scores this way. *She* should have been the one to tell him, especially considering how much impact those scores could have on their relationship. But the confusion left Ty's face almost immediately, and he turned to Amy with a smile.

"So you finally checked your scores, huh?" he said. "How'd you do?"

"I was going to tell you later," she replied in an apologetic tone.

"It's no big deal. Just tell me," Ty encouraged.

By now, Lou had started toward the farmhouse door, and Amy felt a little more in control of the conversation. Still, telling Ty her score felt more significant than he could know. She gazed down at her feet and pushed her hands deep in her pockets. "Thirteen-ten," she answered.

"Excuse me?" Ty asked teasingly. "I didn't hear you. Maybe you should speak up."

Amy rolled her eyes and looked at him. "Thirteen-ten," she repeated, a smile pulling at the edges of her mouth.

"Wow, Amy!" Ty's eyes widened before he grabbed Amy and caught her in a crushing hug. "That's fantastic!" He released one arm but kept the other over her shoulders. "You must feel so accomplished," he said, gazing at her proudly. "I obviously will have to think of ways to keep your mind challenged when you're working around the stable. I don't want you getting bored around here."

Amy couldn't think of a response. First of all, she was

surprised that Ty had no more of a suspicion that Amy was considering college than Lou did. But even more bewildering was Ty's joke about Amy losing interest in Heartland. That couldn't be further from the truth. She still wasn't even sure college was what she wanted, but she was certain that Heartland would always be close to her heart.

"Come on, Ty," she said, turning away to pick up a bag of groceries. "You don't have to do that."

"I know," he assured her. "But I can still be proud of you, can't I?" He gave her a genuine smile as he reached for the remaining bags and closed the trunk.

"I guess so," she said faintly, and then headed toward the house.

✌

Amy left Ty and Lou unpacking the groceries while she wandered out to check on the buckskin gelding. The pony was standing on his own under the trees, staring across the fields. Amy felt very sorry for him. Not only was he sick, he was in a foreign place, and complete strangers were caring for him. She tried calling, but the gelding didn't even look in her direction. Amy climbed the gate and walked across the cold, crisp grass. "Hey, boy," she said softly when she drew near to him.

The pony looked briefly at her and then turned his head to stare deep into the woods again. Amy noticed that his breath still seemed labored, his sides moving more noticeably than she would have expected from a healthy pony.

"Are you lonely, boy?" she asked, reaching her hand up to scratch the pony's neck underneath his mane. With this unexpected cold weather, all of the other horses had been taken in early for the night. Amy glanced up at the heavy clouds that threatened snow although she couldn't believe that would actually happen — not in October.

Amy offered the pony the chopped carrot that she had brought down with her and watched his jawbones working as he began to crunch noisily. "You're a good boy. We'll find your owner soon," she promised, giving him one final pat before heading back to the gate where she could see Joni waiting for her. As she picked her way across the uneven pasture, Amy wondered if Joni had found any remedies for COPD in her mother's books.

"Hi," Joni smiled. "He looks better, doesn't he?"

Amy nodded. "Thanks for everything you've done today. Lou told me that you'd been back and forth between the barn and paddock all day, checking on him."

Joni flipped her long hair over her shoulder. "I found some stuff in your mom's books about COPD and a lot of other stuff. It's totally amazing. Your mom was way ahead of her time. She was like a trailblazer in herbal remedies."

Amy felt a swell of pride as Joni described what she'd read.

"Aloe vera, garlic, and bee pollen tablets are supposed to help with respiratory ailments, and, when a pony's in distress, there is information on an inhaled treatment where you use aloe vera in a nebulizer. But I'd say he doesn't need that at this point," Joni continued with excitement. "I got Ty to drive into town this afternoon and pick up the stuff, and I've given our visitor some of the tablets already," Joni told her.

"Great. Thanks a lot for doing all that, Joni."

"No problem." Joni hesitated. "I hope you don't mind, but I'm kind of calling him Magic. We can't keep calling him the mystery pony, and it's sort of like he appeared out of nowhere — like an old-fashioned conjuring act."

"That's a great idea," Amy said quickly, appreciating the way Joni was able to build an immediate connection with all the horses at Heartland, even the most temporary visitors.

They began to walk up toward the yard. "I got the heavier winter blankets out of the loft this afternoon and stacked them in the feed room just in case we need them," Joni went on. "The weather forecast says that there's going to be a real drop in the temperature tonight."

Amy frowned. "We don't usually get really cold weather this time of year, but it does seem brisk. We'll need to see what it feels like in the barn later," she said hurriedly.

She didn't want Joni thinking she was being ungrateful, but they rarely needed to use blankets before December.

"No problem," Joni said in her trademark laid-back way. "I also put down some rubber matting and washed the inside of one of the stalls in the other block. That way we'll have a place that's free of hay and dust in case it gets too cold to leave Magic out."

"Did you get special permission from Jack to use one of his freshly painted stalls? He won't forgive you if you mess them up!" Amy teased, smiling warmly to let Joni know she was kidding. She felt a surge of gratitude for everything that Joni had done that day while she was in school. "Seriously, that's a great idea. We know it won't trigger Magic's allergy if there's no hay or straw around, and since there aren't any other horses in that block, it should be nice and quiet for him." Amy rubbed her hands together against the cold. "I'm going to check on Spindle before dinner. Would you like to stay and eat with us?"

Joni's face broke into a smile. "Thanks, Amy. I'd love to," she said, cupping her hands in front of her face and blowing into them. "I'm starving! I have a bad feeling that one of the horses ate my lunch! I left my sandwich next to Sundance's stall this morning, and it was gone when I came back."

"Oh, no! Did he at least leave the paper?" Amy felt

the corners of her mouth twitching with amusement. It certainly sounded like one of Sundance's pranks.

Joni grinned. "No! Plastic bag and all. I swear, he must have some goat in him. He can eat anything." Joni grinned.

They walked together into the barn and went straight to Spindleberry's stall, where the colt was pulling at his hay net. "Hey, Spindle," Amy called, holding out a piece of carrot she had saved for him.

Spindle nickered gently and came over to take the carrot. He butted Amy's hand after he had finished. "It's all gone," she told him. She went to scratch his ear and felt a pang of disappointment when the gelding moved away from her to greet Joni.

"Hello, boy." Joni clicked with her tongue and rubbed him between the eyes. "Do you like this cold weather?" she asked. Spindle stood still for a few moments with his eyes half closed before rustling back through the straw to his hay net.

"Oh, that reminds me," Joni said. "I thought I'd found a blanket that would work for Spindle, but I guess I was wrong. There didn't seem to be enough of that size."

"That's weird. I was sure that green one would work for him." Ty's deep voice carried down the aisle. He walked up to Amy, who was still standing by Spindle's door.

"I didn't see an extra green one," Joni replied. "They all had names on them."

Amy wasn't all that concerned. She guessed one of the blankets was stored somewhere else last winter. Instead, she focused on tickling Spindle under the chin.

"I can check in the loft again," Joni offered.

"No, Joni," Amy said. "You've done enough already. You should head inside for dinner. I'll give the loft a quick look." Amy gave Spindle a pat and headed toward the steep wooden staircase in the corner of the building.

"Hang on, I'll go, too. I'm sure I saw a new blanket up there somewhere." Ty caught up with her and went up the stairs first. At the top he turned and offered his hand to help Amy up into the boarded loft space. Amy grasped his gloved hand and stepped into the dusty, low-ceilinged room. The shelf where they kept the blankets was high.

"I bet it's pushed to the back," Ty said, striding over to the storage space. He felt around the dark space with his hand. "I might need a stepladder," he confided.

Amy peered into the dim light provided by the single lightbulb. She wasn't sure if they even had a stepladder up here. As she scanned the cluttered space, something caught her eye. One of the bales of straw had been split and shaken into a soft pile. She didn't remember any of the bales breaking. She walked across the floorboards and crouched down. Bunched up next to the straw was a thick mass of green fabric. It was the very blanket Ty was searching for.

Amy reached for the blanket and glanced back at Ty in disbelief. "Someone has been up here, Ty," she whispered. "And guessing from the warmth of the blanket, they just left."

Chapter Seven

After a quick search of the loft, Ty and Amy decided that whoever had taken refuge must have left. There was not a lot of space in which to hide.

"Do you think it was a homeless person, looking for somewhere warm to sleep?" Amy queried. She felt a pang of sympathy for anyone who had to sleep outdoors. Despite what she had said to Joni earlier, the cold of the October night was sharp and the wind was strong.

"That's a possibility, but my guess is we won't ever find out. Whoever it was is probably long gone." Ty gave the green blanket a quick shake and flung it over his shoulder.

Amy picked up a crumpled brown bag from the floor. "At least this solves the mystery of Joni's lunch. I'm relieved that it wasn't Sundance's fault. If he's not care-

94

ful, he could be fighting colic again." Amy had meant her comment to be a joke, but it just hung in the air. The loft felt foreign, knowing someone else had been there recently. Amy crumpled the brown bag into a smaller ball and stuffed it into her coat pocket.

"Come on," Ty offered. "We should finish up and head inside. Do you want Spindle to wear this blanket?"

Amy thought he'd be warm enough in the barn, so she just shook her head. "But maybe we should take advantage of the stall Joni cleaned and bring Magic in. I don't want him out if it gets much colder."

❧

Next morning, Amy could feel the change in temperature the moment she threw off her covers. She peered out her bedroom window, but it was too dark to make out whether it had snowed in the night. She decided to dress in layers for extra warmth, finishing with a thick woolen red sweater over long underwear and jeans.

As soon as Amy walked into the kitchen, she snapped on the light switch and crossed over to the thermostat to turn up the dial. "It's freezing," she muttered to herself, thinking of Lou's wedding in three days' time. She couldn't imagine how inconvenient it would be if it snowed. When she pondered the muddy pathways and slick, icy driveway, Amy couldn't help but feel that her sister and Scott should have waited for a summer wedding.

She put the kettle on and turned on the radio for company while she made some toast. It was still early as far as the horses were concerned, and she couldn't face going out into the freezing cold until she'd had something to eat. She reached into the fridge for the marmalade before sitting down at the table with her plate and a steaming cup of coffee. As Amy ate her breakfast, she began to draw up a list of everything that would have to be done in the stables while she was at school today. For one thing, she'd have to ask Ty to call McDermott's, the feed supplier, to increase the grain delivery just in case they did get snow. Amy imagined Lou would be too distracted by the wedding to think of that detail.

Finishing her last mouthful of toast, Amy pushed back her chair and carried her plate and cup to the sink. She wanted to give Magic some of the garlic and bee pollen tablets that Joni had mentioned the previous day. Amy pulled on a fleecy jacket, her scarf, and a hat, but she still shuddered at the bitter cold of the air when she opened the door. She was surprised to see, in the half-light, Joni's car already parked. Joni was sitting in the front seat with her legs dangling out. It took Amy a minute to realize that she was pulling on thick rubber yard boots. Amy assumed it was part of Joni's winter garb. The Canadian stable hand no doubt knew how to be properly outfitted for freezing weather.

Amy waved. "You're early!"

"I figured if we did get snow later on, there'd be some extra work to do," Joni called back cheerfully. Amy waited until she was ready and then they both headed around to the stable block to check on the dappled buckskin before seeing to the horses in the barn.

Amy admired the stable block with its fresh coat of treated paint as she reached up to tug at the bolts on the top half of the stable door. Joni helped her swing back the door and secure it before they looked into the stall.

Amy frowned. She could sense something was wrong even before the terrible sound of wheezing reached her ears. "He's sick again!" she exclaimed, fumbling at the lower bolt in panic. After two clumsy attempts, she managed to pull back the bolt and hurry inside as Joni hit the light switch. Magic was standing in the far corner, his neck lathered with sweat. Before Amy reached him, he went into a spasm of hacking coughs. She ran her hand down his wet neck, feeling panic rise inside her. "I don't know what's wrong," she said in a trembling voice. "There's no dust in here. Something else must be triggering the reaction."

"Do you want me to call Scott?" Joni offered, her eyes wide with concern as she looked at the stream of discharge dripping from Magic's nose.

"Yes, but we have to do something else first," Amy pointed out. "He's much worse than yesterday. We need to get him out of here. He got better yesterday once he was outside in the paddock."

"OK."

"If you take him, I'll go get the remedies and phone Scott." Amy crossed the stall swiftly and reached toward the hook outside to get the halter and lead rope.

Joni took the halter from Amy and slipped it over the gelding's head.

As Amy raced away, she could hear the pony launch into another spell of rasping coughs. When she reached the feed room, she clicked on the kettle they kept on the counter. She grabbed the bottle of aloe vera and rummaged in a box on the top shelf for the nebulizer that she knew was there. Glancing at her mom's open notebook, she measured the aloe vera into the container and then added hot water. Her fingers were clumsy as she screwed the cap down. She was dizzy with worry about Magic, so she went by instinct in putting the nebulizer together to save time. Her mind raced, trying to identify what had set off the pony's symptoms. She was sure Joni had eliminated all dust from that stall.

Amy rushed down to the field with the nebulizer under her arm. She used her free hand to dial Scott's number on her cell phone. She bit her lip in frustration when she was transferred to his voice mail. Amy left a hurried message before tucking the phone back into her pocket and breaking into a sprint. Joni had tied Magic just inside the gate. Like the day before, his whole body sagged and his sides heaved in and out with each labored breath.

"Good job getting him here," Amy gasped as she climbed over the gate. Joni nodded and watched Amy reach her arm under the pony's head and at the same time fit the nebulizer mask over his mouth.

"Here," Joni said, slipping the container into position. Amy looked at the contraption to figure out what went where. She quickly screwed the long breathing hose onto the mask. Now the light mist of aloe vera should flow from the hot-water vestibule, through the hose, and to the mask. The mask covered the pony's muzzle, so he breathed in a concentration of the aloe.

It was a while before either girl spoke. They watched the forlorn pony stand motionless with the odd contraption strapped to his head. "You know, I'm sure his breathing is already easing up," Joni said, taking a step so she could see Magic's sides. Her brow furrowed as she moved in and listened to the sound of the gelding taking each painful breath.

Amy listened, too. "You could be right."

"It just doesn't make sense," Joni said, puzzled. "I was sure he'd be OK after I scrubbed down the walls."

Amy glanced at Joni's pale face. "I'm sure it wasn't

dust," she reassured her. "There must be something else he is allergic to. But what? I don't think it was his feed."

The pony gave a deep, hollow-sounding sigh and adjusted his weight so he was leaning against Amy. "Don't worry, boy," she told him, slipping her hand through his mane. "We'll figure it out, I promise."

❧

By the time Ty's car appeared in the driveway, Magic's breathing was steady. Amy felt it was safe to leave him on his own in the paddock until Scott arrived, and she agreed with Joni that someone should check Magic every fifteen or twenty minutes.

When she reached the yard, Ty was crouching down by the Jeep that Jack kept for heavier work on the farm. Amy saw that he was placing chains over the tires. "Hey," he said without looking around. "Lou just told me McDermott's called. They canceled our grain delivery because of the snow forecast. I'm going to pick up some extra feed just in case. We don't want to be running short close to the wedding. I'll get some sand, too, in case the yard gets icy." His voice was muffled by the clinking of the tire chains. "And," he added, giving Amy a half smile, "Lou asked me to tell you to stay home from school today. She doesn't want to worry about you getting stranded."

Amy gave a wry laugh. "Are you kidding?" Usually

she was the one trying to persuade Lou to let her stay home from school, not vice versa.

"So," Ty said as he slowly got to his feet, brushing his hands on his jeans, "where were you guys when I got here?"

"Magic got sick again last night," Amy told him, watching his contented expression change to one of concern. "Joni will explain. I need to call Scott to see how long he's going to be."

In the kitchen, Jack was on the phone. Amy washed her hands while she waited for him to finish. Jack caught her attention when he said, "Thanks for letting us know, Sergeant." Amy's heart quickened. Maybe there was news about Magic's owner!

Jack hung up the phone and turned to Amy with a quizzical look on his face. "Well," he said, scratching the side of his cheek. "That was the police. They've passed on some information about the pony."

"They found his owner?" she guessed eagerly as Lou walked into the room.

"Did we track down the owner?" Lou echoed, catching the last part of the conversation.

"Yes and no," Jack answered.

Amy sighed, wondering what her grandpa meant by this vague statement. She impatiently scuffed her foot back and forth over the kitchen rug.

Jack pulled out a chair and sat down. "A pony matching

the description of the one that arrived here has been reported missing."

"That's great." Amy felt a surge of relief wash over her. "So when do his owners want to pick him up?"

Jack looked grave. "It's not that easy. The owner of the pony is missing, too. A nine-year-old boy called Evan. His foster parents, Mr. and Mrs. Holloway, are beside themselves with worry."

Amy felt her heart skip a beat. "You know who that is, don't you?" Lou and Jack looked at her in surprise. "He was here the day before yesterday. He was with the guy who delivered the bay trees!"

"No!" Lou exclaimed. "That's awful."

Amy quickly connected Evan's disappearance and the misplaced lunch and blanket, and she filled in Lou and Jack. It had never occurred to her that someone might have purposely brought the pony there to Heartland, but as the puzzle pieces fell into place, that seemed to be the most likely scenario.

"Do you think he's still here, Amy?" Lou crossed the room to join them at the table with a fresh mug of coffee.

"I don't know," Amy confessed. "He wasn't in the hayloft, that's for sure." Her stomach churned at the thought of Evan hiding away somewhere in the bitter cold. She drummed her fingers on the tabletop as her sister began to dial the number of the Holloways. Amy tried to think through all the possible places he could hide.

The door opened and Ty poked his head into the kitchen. "Scott's here to look at Magic."

"You go, Amy," Lou cupped her hand over the phone. "If they don't answer, I'll call the police. I'll let you know if there's any news."

❧

Amy jogged down to the field and met Scott as he was returning from the paddock. "He seems much better now," the vet told her. "The nebulizer must have done the trick." He glanced up at the heavy clouds and hesitated before saying, "I think it's going to be best to keep him out in the paddock. Just make sure he's got another blanket."

As they began to walk back to the house, Amy explained the precautions they had taken before stabling the pony the night before. "Joni cleaned all the walls, and we didn't feed him any hay." Amy frowned. "Is it possible that he's allergic to something else?"

"He must be. I could come back later today and do an allergy test on him," Scott suggested as they reached his Jeep. He turned to face Amy, cupping his hands over his mouth and blowing into them. "You know, you'd make a great diagnostician."

"Really?" Amy narrowed her eyes to see if he was pulling her leg, but his expression was serious.

"Really. Because you don't just go by the physical

evidence, you also have incredible intuition when it comes to horses," he went on.

Amy paused to take in what her future brother-in-law had said. She realized that Lou would have told Scott about her SAT score, and it looked like Scott was the only person at Heartland who thought she might have more career options now.

"I haven't made any decisions yet about what I want to do," Amy said, dropping her gaze to the floor and picking a piece of hay off her coat.

"It's OK, I'd never pressure you into following my career path. My parents do enough of that for our whole family." Scott let out a laugh, then shook his head. "But if you did, you'd be a natural. I'm willing to bet on it."

❧

Ty followed Scott out of the driveway, on his way to pick up the feed and sand. Amy and Joni were left to fill extra hay nets since they were leaving the horses in the barn. Amy couldn't keep thoughts of Evan out of her mind as she collected another blanket from the loft and went outside to put it on Magic.

Her breath left a stream of vapor in the air. It was so cold! Colder than any October she could remember. As she lifted up her head to the gray sky, she felt the lightest icy sensation touch her nose. It was followed by another on her cheek and then another. Snow! Amy turned up her coat collar and went past Joni, who was taking the last wheelbarrow load out to the muck pile. Amy had to blink the snow off her eyelashes as she said to Joni, "I'm just going to go put this blanket on Magic."

"OK," Joni agreed. "I'll put this away," she nodded at the wheelbarrow, "and then come and help you."

At that moment there was a banging on the kitchen window and Amy saw Lou beckoning to her. "I can take the blanket if you want," Joni offered.

"Thanks," Amy said, handing it over and hurrying toward the house as Lou opened the door. A middle-aged couple hovered just behind her, and Amy recognized the man who had delivered the bay trees.

"Chris and Janet Holloway are here," Lou said. "Could you show them the pony?"

"Sure," Amy said, feeling a pang of sympathy at the desperate expression on their faces. "He's in the field."

Lou stood back for Chris and Janet to make their way out the door. Janet Holloway was much shorter than her husband and, up close, Amy could see deep lines of worry around her eyes and mouth. Janet pushed a strand of brown hair behind her ear and then took Chris's gloved hand in her own. They exchanged a silent look filled with such private emotion that Amy felt awkward witnessing it.

The moment the Holloways set eyes on Magic, Janet gripped Chris's arm.

"That's him. That's Tiger," Chris Holloway said.

"Tiger," Amy echoed. She had almost forgotten that Magic wasn't his real name.

Chris cleared his throat. "A friend of ours gave him to us a few months ago. It was just after Evan came to live with us. We own a pasture and a little two-stall barn. When Sheila moved, she asked if we would keep Tiger with our old mare."

"Did you know he was suffering from a respiratory condition?" Amy asked.

"Yes, we did." Janet answered this time. "But Sheila assured us that it was under control. He was fine all summer because we kept him out, but then when we started to bring him in for the cold nights last week, he went downhill."

"To make matters worse, our dog got sick at the same time, and we had to put him down." Chris tore his gaze away from Tiger and looked at Amy. "It was the best thing. He was in a lot of pain, and because he was in distress, he was panting all the time."

At first, Amy thought it was an odd thing for Chris to say. She thought he was just rambling, but then she made the connection. "You know," Amy broke in excitedly, "Evan told me about Rusty — he was really upset.

He must have made a connection to Tiger's breathing when he has an attack."

"Exactly." Chris put his arm around Janet, who rubbed her eyes wearily. He took a deep breath. "He must have assumed we would put Tiger down, and that explains why we're here."

Amy thought back to her conversation with the little boy. She remembered talking about how they treated horses at Heartland. Amy guessed that Evan thought they could make Tiger better. She felt a pang of guilt. "It's all my fault," she said miserably. "He thought we'd be able to cure him, and if anything, we made him worse."

Chris ran a hand over his thinning brown hair. "It's no one's fault. You couldn't have known that Evan would run away," he told her.

"None of that matters now," Janet broke in. "Do you have any idea where he is? We've got to find him soon. He already has a cold, and I'm really scared that if we don't find him, it will turn into something worse." With that, Janet tried to snuff back her tears and covered her face with her hands.

"We'll find him," Chris said, putting his arm around her. "Don't you worry. We'll find Evan."

Chapter Eight

❧

Amy quickly told the Holloways all of the events since Tiger's arrival, and they talked about where Evan might have gone after leaving the loft. The Holloways wanted to search the area and try to convince Evan that Tiger was safe so he would come out of hiding.

"OK, if you cover the fields that border the woods along Clairdale Ridge," Amy suggested, "I can go inside and recruit people to check the far pasture and all the buildings."

Amy stayed long enough to let Chris and Janet out of the paddock, and then she sprinted back to the house. She burst into the kitchen, which was empty. *Where is everyone?* she thought, frustrated. She checked the living room before going to Lou's office. To her relief, her sister was studying her computer screen, gnawing her thumbnail.

"It's a good thing I have a manicure appointment," she said ruefully, glancing up at Amy. She pushed her hand through her hair. "Is everything OK? Was it their pony?"

"Yes," Amy said in a rush. "But they're really worried about Evan. They're pretty sure he's somewhere close by. They don't think he'd desert the pony. I told them we'd all go out and shout for him. Can you find Grandpa and cover the side and back fields? I'll ask Joni to check around the yard again, then I'll go to the start of the trails and call around there."

"Sure." Lou pushed out her chair and swung her legs out from under her desk. "Grandpa went to Nancy's, but of course I'll help."

Amy was on her way outside when she remembered the most important part. "Hey, Lou?" she called. "Just make sure you shout that Tiger's going to be OK. Evan will keep hiding if he thinks something could happen to him."

❧

Amy stood at the bottom of the path that led up to Teak's Hill, scanning the horizon and squinting to try to see through the mass of bare brown trees. She cupped her gloved hands over her mouth and yelled for Evan. Her words echoed faintly through the tunnel of trees as she listened for a reply. When she opened her mouth to call again, a whirl of wind blew snowflakes into her mouth. As she stood there, the snow started to accumulate on the ground and on the topside of the tree limbs.

The cold crept into her joints, and she wondered how long a child could survive in these conditions. "Evan," she yelled again, her hopes sinking further each time she called his name. She made her way up to the first fork in the trail, stopping every few feet to listen for a response. Following the other trail back down to the yard, Amy yelled less frequently, her throat aching from the frozen air.

She walked back to the yard and saw the Holloways talking to Tiger over the paddock fence. Hearing her approach, they looked up, and she could only shake her head in response to their questioning eyes.

"Nothing, I'm sorry," she told them. She was the last one to return. Joni and Lou were standing a little farther down the fence. Their cheeks and noses were bright red from the icy wind.

"We're going to have to get home," said Chris, taking his wife's arm. "The police are already out searching, but our friends are organizing a search party, too. We'll tell them that Tiger is here, and we'll probably come back and use this as a starting point."

"Thanks for your help," Janet added as they turned back to their car.

"If we can do anything else, just give us a call," Lou called. "Let us know when you come back, and we'll head out with you."

Chris raised his hand before they both climbed into the car and pulled slowly out of the yard.

Amy suddenly realized that her cell phone was ringing. She reached into her pocket and fished it out, her gloved hands clumsy, as Lou and Joni headed into the house.

"It's me," Ty's deep voice said at the other end. "No one's answering the house phone."

"We've all been outside." Amy quickly brought him up to date regarding Tiger, Evan, and the Holloways as she walked to the barn.

"The poor kid," said Ty. "He can't be far. As soon as I get back, I'll go out in the Jeep and look for him."

"Good idea," Amy said.

"What?" Ty raised his voice. "Amy, I can't hear you."

A crackle of static broke through the line, and Amy guessed that the inclement weather was probably breaking up the signal.

"Amy?" he asked.

"I'm here," she enunciated, trying to get through the fuzz.

"Look, McDermott's is out of feed." His voice came through in choppy phrases. "Everyone had the same idea, and there's been a rush. I'm going across town to the other feed store. I'll come straight home from there."

Amy paused to make sure he was done. "Be careful," she said. "The weather is getting ugly." Amy leaned back against the wall. The static had increased. She wanted to tell him that Scott was planning to do an allergy test on Tiger, but she had a feeling they wouldn't have their connection that long.

"Amy, I'm losing you." Ty's voice began breaking up.

"I'll see you when you get back," Amy said quickly. "Drive safely." But the line had already gone dead.

Ty's words stuck with Amy, and she was sure he was right. With Tiger at Heartland, Amy was certain that Evan would not have gone very far. As the snow came down, a burning feeling was slowly building inside Amy, a mixture of adrenaline and determination. She stood up and looked out through the double doors of the barn. Snow was falling heavily, a swirling white curtain that blurred everything in sight. Amy knew she couldn't wait for Ty to get back with the Jeep. In this weather, there would not be a lot of time. She needed to act now.

There was no doubt that four legs would be faster than two, so Amy headed back to the tack room for Sundance's saddle and bridle. As she reached for the saddle, she realized she needed to be prepared. She first went to the small desk underneath the bridle hooks. She opened a drawer and pulled out pen and paper to write Joni a quick note. Then she hurried to the other side of the room and stacked a waterproof sheet and woolen stable blanket on top of the saddle.

🙠

"It's OK, boy." Amy patted the gelding's warm neck as he hesitated in the snow. Sundance had been very willing until he stepped into the snow that measured well above his fetlocks. Amy's nose was already freezing. Each snowflake was an icy prick on her skin. She couldn't blame Sundance for preferring the warmth of his stall. Pulling her scarf up over her face, she pushed Sundance forward. With a toss of his head, he picked his way carefully over the icy concrete, his neck arched and his head held low. Amy felt bad that she was taking Sundance out in weather like this, but finding Evan took priority over everything else. And if she could pick any horse that would have the heart for this kind of rescue mission, Sundance would always be at the top of her list.

As soon as Sundance's hooves hit the trail, he began to move with more confidence. Amy had packed his feet with grease to stop them from filling with snow, and Sundance was clearly relieved that his legs seemed solid beneath him.

Amy tried shouting for Evan as she went, but her words were snatched away by the wind. She concentrated instead on keeping Sundance going. The snow stung her eyes, and she could barely see; the trees lining the path were a gray blur. To her surprise Sundance suddenly veered off to the left instead of pressing up the hill. Amy corrected him, angling him toward the main path by squeezing on the opposite rein. Sundance's pace shortened, and it took Amy a while to realize that Sundance had tried to take the path they had ridden along the last time they were out. It seemed so long ago that they had tackled the new cross-country jumping course. Amy could barely make out where the ground was through the driving snow. She couldn't imagine trying to take on jumps.

Amy wiped her hands over her eyes. "Come on, boy," she shouted. "Stick to the trail." Sundance pinned his ears against his head but continued plowing up the hill, his progress painfully slow.

They rode on against the wind for a few more moments when an idea came to Amy. She had not thought of it when Sundance first hesitated at the other path, but now she could not put it out of her mind. She brought Sundance to a halt and turned him toward Heartland. Sensing he was nearing the end of his outing, Sundance picked up the pace, moving steadily down the hill with the wind at his back. But when Amy pulled on the right rein to turn the gelding off the main trail, Sundance resisted. "Please, Sunny, just for me," she said, leaning forward to shake the snow from his mane. "Come on, boy. Evan needs us."

Amy could feel Sundance relax, and as they turned along the path, Amy pushed him into a trot. They jumped over the tree trunk, and she kept Sundance trotting as they approached the stream. It was frozen now with a gathering layer of snow. One of Sundance's front hooves faltered, skimming across an icy patch, but the pony collected himself for a broad leap across the still brook. With the momentum, Sundance broke into a canter, and as he did, a bright splash of blue caught Amy's eye. She circled Sundance and trotted back along the path until she located the spot of color. It was a mitten. Amy's heart skipped ahead, and she spun Sundance around in the snow. The mitten was not yet covered by snow. There might still be time.

Sundance picked up a canter and bolted ahead through the snow. He gathered himself for the picket fence. As soon as he cleared it, Amy slipped down from the saddle before he had even stopped trotting. She threw the reins over a post that stood next to the front of the old shed. As Amy ran to the worn wooden door, she knew it was a long shot. The door was splintered and hanging off its hinges.

"Evan," she called. "Evan, are you here?" She pulled on the door and stood on the threshold as her eyes adjusted to the darkness. "Evan?" she called again, and her heart missed a beat as she rushed toward a shape slumped in the corner of the room.

"Evan." She gasped, dropping to her knees and putting her hand on the boy's shoulder. Until this point, she had not considered the fact that she might be too late. "Evan, it's Amy. You have to wake up!"

Chapter Nine

❧

Amy held her breath while she listened for a sound from the little boy. Just as she felt a weighty sorrow fall over her, a low, gurgling sound emanated from his chest.

Amy's shoulders sagged with relief. "Evan, I'll be right back. You're going to be OK." She instinctively gave him a hug, rose to her feet, and hurried back to the door.

Sundance was standing with his head bowed against the driving snow, his eyes closed. Amy reached toward his withers to peel back the protective weatherproof sheet. She next unfastened the buckles that held the rolled-up blanket to the saddle, her fingers trembling. She held the blanket between her knees as she carefully pulled the sheet back across Sundance. She gave him a pat that swept a dense layer of wet flakes to the ground before tracing her own footsteps back to the shed.

Amy tucked the blanket around Evan and then peeled off her gloves and took his hands in hers. They were colder than the dirt floor she was kneeling on. Amy began briskly rubbing his small hands between her own to try to warm them. She decided it might be less disorienting for Evan if she held his hands in her own, squeezing gently from time to time.

"Come on, Evan," she urged. "Open your eyes." Amy could hear he was fighting to breathe, but his lack of response was starting to frighten her. She wasn't sure what was worse, the painful rasp of each stifled breath or the silence that followed. In every still moment, she prayed to herself.

As she put her hand on Evan's forehead, Amy remembered that she had a miniature flashlight on her key ring. *Please, please let me have it,* she hoped. She pushed her hands into the deep pockets of her insulated jacket and felt around. In the right-hand pocket, her fingers slid around the pencil-thin tool nestled among her keys. Amy pulled out the ring with a clatter, and she twisted the top of the miniature tool to turn on a narrow beam of light. She gazed in dismay at the whiteness of Evan's face. Shadowed with dark blue undertones, it looked fragile and pale. Even his freckles were drained of color. Picturing him when he first visited Heartland, Amy could hardly believe it had been just a few days since she had seen him full of energy and curiosity. It felt as if it had been much longer.

Amy thrust her hand back into her pocket and pulled out her cell phone. She pressed the speed dial to call home. "C'mon," Amy muttered. "Someone be there. Please!"

The line clicked but Amy couldn't make out a voice over the crackling. "Hello?" She raised her voice. "I can't hear you. Hello!" The line fuzzed again, and then, to her amazement, she heard Matt's voice quite clearly.

"Amy?" He sounded concerned. "Amy, are you OK? Lou's freaking out. Joni found your note about ten minutes ago, and Lou panicked. Scott and I came over to . . ."

"Matt!" Amy interrupted. "I found him! I found Evan. I need help!"

"Where? What's wrong?"

"Listen. I've only got Sundance. Someone with four-wheel drive has to get up here. Evan's not responding. He's so cold, Matt." She took a deep, shaky breath. "Is Ty back?"

"No, I haven't seen him. Amy, just do what you can to make him warm. Keep talking to him, and we'll get to you as soon as possible. I need directions. Where are you?"

Amy quickly described the route, explaining how Matt could come from the road on Clairdale Ridge to limit his time on the dirt paths. Amy hoped the trails would be wide enough for a vehicle. When she remembered the fences across the path she reached to call Matt back, but thought again when she realized the snow would have them well covered by now.

Amy turned her attention back to Evan. "Evan, listen to me. You need to wake up. Our vet is at Heartland right now with Tiger. We think we can make him better! Evan, please wake up. Tiger needs you."

There was still no response from the young boy, but Amy was encouraged when his eyelids flickered at the sound of Tiger's name. Amy tucked the blanket more securely around Evan before taking his hands again. With stiff fingers she tried to put her gloves on Evan's hands. It took her ages, and she kept talking to him as she fumbled to pull the fabric over his clenched fists. "Tiger's such a good pony. You must be so proud of him. I know he was in bad shape, but we're going to find out what's making him sick and then we can make him better, I promise. So you've got to pull through, too, Evan. Because Tiger will be waiting for you." Amy blinked back desperate tears. She felt helpless. Looking at Evan, she had no idea what to do.

Please hurry, Matt. I don't know if he'll make it. She moved closer to him, hoping her own body heat would help. And then Evan stirred, trying to run his tongue over his chapped lips.

"Evan," Amy said urgently. "Can you hear me?"

She waited, holding her breath, as the little boy became still once more. Amy lowered her head and strained to see if she could hear a car making its way to the shed. At first she heard nothing, but then there was the tiniest sound. A whisper.

"Tiger."

Amy opened her eyes. "Evan!" she exclaimed. "Yes, Tiger is at Heartland." Instinctively, Amy started to tell Evan how great it would be for him to ride Tiger again. She described how her favorite thing was to take Sundance on the trails, and that they had jumped along the path outside before the snow. Trying to inspire Evan, Amy talked him through the course stride by stride. "Once you're both better, you can come to Heartland and ride the trails. We can race along together under the trees, leaping over logs. Imagine how much fun it will be. You just have to get better, and we'll go for that ride, I promise."

She didn't know how long she kept talking, but the cold air had dried her mouth and her voice was cracking when she heard the sound of an engine churning through the snow. "Help's here, Evan. Just hold on. You're going to be OK." A flood of relief washed over her as voices approached the shack, and then there were footsteps across the floor and the incredibly comforting realization that she was no longer alone with Evan.

"Hey, Evan. How are you doing? My name's Matt,

and I know you're having a good time with Amy," he said, crouching down by the boy's head, "but it would be good to move the party somewhere warmer."

Amy looked at Matt in shock. Here he was, wearing the same black winter jacket he wore to school. Somehow, Amy had expected Scott to come. She knew she had talked to Matt on the phone, but she thought an adult would come to the rescue, someone like Scott, who arrived at Heartland in times of need and provided answers and reassurance. Amy felt the shadows of doubt return, but there was something in Matt's voice that sounded like his older brother. His tone was even and light. He grinned at Amy before going on. "How does that sound, Evan?"

He glanced at Amy. "Can you help me get Evan's jeans off? They're soaked through. He's better off without them, just wrapped in the blanket." Amy nodded and bent down to help.

"Can I do something?" a worried voice sounded from the doorway. Just then realizing Joni was there, Amy turned and gave her a weak smile.

"I think that Evan is in the early stages of hypothermia," Matt explained. "He's listless and his lips are blue. As long as we can get him dry and warm, he should be just fine. Right, Evan?" Matt added, clearly aware that the little boy could hear every word even though his eyes remained shut. Concentrating on pulling at Evan's wet pant leg, he glanced at Joni, who remained by the door. "Joni, can you call nine-one-one and have them contact the hospital, so they're ready for us? Then call Lou, and she can be in touch with Evan's foster parents."

Joni nodded and stepped out of the shed.

"Can you also open the back door of the Jeep for me?" Matt called. "Amy and I will carry Evan out." He shot a look at Amy, who was just finishing with her side of Evan's pants. Matt took a deep breath before saying, "We need to keep Evan in a horizontal position, OK?" Amy thought that would make it harder to carry him, but she trusted Matt. He seemed so calm and confident, as if he rescued unconscious children from snowbound sheds on a monthly basis. She was relieved that he was the one who had answered the phone at Heartland.

"Evan, I'm sorry you won't get an ambulance ride out of this," Matt said as he slipped his arm gently behind Evan's head, careful not to bump it against the wall. "I have a feeling an emergency vehicle would have had trouble getting up here in the snow." He shifted so he could place his hands underneath Evan's armpits and then nodded at Amy to take the boy's legs.

On Matt's count of three, Amy lifted them up, surprised at how light Evan was. As they carried him out into the fading light, Evan's eyelids flickered again and he opened his eyes. When Amy helped Matt to lift the boy onto the backseat of the Jeep, she met his frightened gaze. "You'll be all right," she murmured.

Joni hurried over the snow, her boots making a loud crunching sound. "I'll take Sundance home," she told Amy. Her cheeks were bright red with cold. "I've called ahead to the hospital, and they're expecting you in the emergency room."

Amy impulsively reached out to give Joni a hug. "Thanks," she said, appreciating her new friend's generosity more than ever.

Joni smiled and gave her hand a quick squeeze before standing back to shut the door. Amy stayed in the back, kneeling on the floor and facing Evan. Matt had left the engine running and the Jeep was filled with warm air, making Amy's nose tingle. As Matt put the Jeep into reverse, Amy took one last proud look at Sundance, whose coat was covered in a light layer of snow. She knew he would be safe going back with Joni.

Amy stroked Evan's forehead while the Jeep rattled along as fast as Matt could safely go. "There's a thermos of hot chocolate on the floor," Matt told her, his eyes briefly meeting hers in the rearview mirror. "I kind of took it off Heartland's stove. I hope no one misses it," he said, smiling. "Do you think you can give some to Evan, if you prop his head up a little? And you should have some, too. You look frozen."

Amy looked at her reflection, wincing at her bright red nose and watery eyes, before methodically reaching down for the thermos. She realized she was following Matt's instructions without questioning them, taking comfort in his certainty. *Matt was born to be a doctor,* she thought.

As she helped Evan to sip the chocolate, Matt explained that he had gone to Heartland with Scott to set up some gas-powered heaters to thaw out the lawn so the tent could be set up the following day. The company claimed they would not come out unless they had a guarantee that the ground was not frozen solid. When Matt got to the part about not having a chance to tell Scott he was taking the Jeep, Amy was surprised. Matt explained that his brother was busy in the paddock taking blood samples from Tiger. "And I knew that was for a good cause," Matt said. Amy could tell by his voice that he was smiling.

"Did you hear that, Evan? Scott is running tests so we can find out what's making Tiger sick." Amy felt a motherly rush of relief that the boy's lips were returning to a pinkish hue and his complexion was less pale.

They drove along in silence for a while. Suddenly, a hoarse, thin voice said, "I ran away . . . so scared."

Amy looked down to see Evan's blue eyes firmly fixed on her. "You ran away because you were scared?" Amy questioned. When Evan nodded, she continued. "Were you scared that Tiger wouldn't get well?" she prompted, resting her hand on his forehead.

Evan gave the tiniest nod. "Then," Evan started before taking a big breath, "I thought I was going to get found in your barn and get in trouble."

Amy's heart tugged toward the little boy, and she quickly reassured him that he wasn't in any trouble. "Your foster parents aren't angry. They were just really scared you'd get sick," she told him.

To her surprise, Evan managed a smile. "They always worry." His voice was drowsy and his eyelids began to droop, flittering between being open and closed. "They don't need to," he added. "I can take care of myself."

Amy was silent for a moment and then she said quietly, "They love you very much. And that's a good thing." She stared back out the window, not really seeing the snow-laden trees or the passing vehicles. "I used to have someone like that. It made me feel special to have someone love me so much." Evan's eyes were now fully closed, and Amy's thoughts were of her mother and remembering how she, too, had been overprotective at times. But as Amy got older, her mother had trusted her more and more to take care of herself and make decisions for herself. Even so, her presence was all the comfort Amy had ever needed. By the time Amy looked back down at Evan, the little boy was asleep, his chest rising and falling with a soft wheezing sound.

She met Matt's eyes again in the mirror. She put her hands together and rested her head on them, indicating that Evan had fallen asleep. Matt nodded at her in understanding before quietly announcing, "We're here." Matt put on his signal and turned into the emergency room entrance. He pulled up to the curb and almost immediately they were swept up in a rush of activity, with medics carefully sliding Evan from the backseat onto a gurney. The Holloways were there, too, looking pale but relieved. Janet, tears shining in her eyes, bent down to give Evan a swift kiss before he was pushed through the open glass doors and into the hospital. Then she looked up at Amy and mouthed the words "thank you" before Chris hurried her inside.

As Matt stopped one of the paramedics to tell her the specifics, Amy felt the last bit of adrenaline drain from her, and she leaned back against Scott's Jeep feeling utterly exhausted.

She pulled herself back to reality when Matt put his hand on her arm. "Are you OK?"

Amy was suddenly aware of her exhaustion, her damp clothes, and her runny nose. "I feel kind of like a piece of soggy cardboard," she admitted.

"That's a funny image, but I understand," Matt replied with a laugh. "Come on, let me park the Jeep and then we'll go to the hospital cafeteria to warm up. I'll treat you to a coffee before we head home."

Once they were settled at a table, Amy cupped her hands around the steaming mug and realized that Evan was still wearing her riding gloves. She half smiled at the thought before looking up at Matt, who was stirring his coffee with a spoon. "You were incredible," she told him. "The way you just swooped in and knew what to do. I was about to give up."

To her amusement, a reddish tinge crept over Matt's face. "I don't think 'incredible' is altogether accurate. I think I seemed more composed than I felt," he said humbly. "But," he hesitated, "this is going to sound awful, but once I knew Evan was going to be OK, I kind of started enjoying myself."

"It doesn't sound awful," Amy reassured him, knowing just what he meant. "I get the same rush when I'm working with horses. As long as I know they're going to get better, I get really into it."

"You know, helping him was pretty amazing. Seeing his color return and hearing him talk to you. Knowing that I helped make that happen — I don't think I'll ever forget it." Matt looked directly at Amy. "It made me realize for the first time that it's not my parents' dream for me to become a doctor — it's mine."

Amy reached her hands across the table to cover Matt's. "That's so great!" she exclaimed. "Now it's my turn to confess," Amy announced with a teasing smile. "It was all a scheme! It was an evil ploy to get you to recognize your true calling! Evan is really an aspiring child actor."

"Yeah, right." Matt grinned self-consciously and leaned back in his chair, putting his arms behind his head. "I'd be flattered if you went to the trouble, but I think I know just enough about hypothermia to know that wasn't blue lipstick on Evan's mouth."

Amy smiled, a little astonished at how easy it was to laugh when just a short while ago, things had been so serious.

"And what about you, Miss Fleming? Have you decided how you will put your considerable talents to use after graduation?" Although Matt's tone was teasing, Amy knew she could not joke her way out of this one. Matt wanted an honest answer.

Amy hesitated. "I guess I've come to a decision, yes. I think when I graduate, it might be best if I didn't go straight into working at Heartland full-time." She took a deep breath. "I think I want to apply for the prevet program."

Chapter Ten

❧

On the ride home, Amy insisted again and again that she didn't want Matt to tell anyone else that she was thinking about college.

"I hear you," Matt said, his tone heavy with mock exasperation.

Amy couldn't help grinning. "Sorry, have I mentioned it already?"

"Just once or twice."

They fell into silence and Amy leaned her head against the glass, thinking of the relief on the Holloways' faces as they thanked her and Matt for saving Evan. The little boy was already recovering from his ordeal and was going to stay at the hospital overnight before being released to go back home.

Amy wondered how Tiger was, forced to be out in the snowy paddock. "At least it's stopped snowing," she commented aloud. "Hopefully, it will all melt before Saturday. I think it would be beautiful if Heartland was a winter wonderland for the wedding."

"But I bet your sister could name a thousand reasons why it would be a logistical catastrophe," Matt said with a smile.

"No tent, for one," Amy offered.

"Thanks for reminding me," Matt answered. "I still have to defrost the lawn before the tent guys arrive."

"Not much chance of that now," Amy remarked. It had been dark by the time they had left the hospital. After the storm, the roads were quiet, with only an occasional pair of headlights sweeping into the Jeep as they drove back.

"I'll have to come back tomorrow," Matt agreed. As he turned into Heartland's driveway, he added, "Don't let yourself be talked out of being a vet, Amy, if that's what you really feel you want to do."

Amy felt a jolt of surprise. "I don't think anyone would try to talk me out of it," she protested. But her tone wasn't convincing — not even to her own ears.

"No, but I doubt there's anyone looking forward to seeing you go."

"I wouldn't want them to!" Amy said defensively, but

she knew her reaction had much deeper roots. Matt was too close to the truth. She couldn't shake the feelings of disappointment that no one in her family seemed to suspect her ambition, her new hopes for herself.

Matt carefully drove the Jeep up the drive. The headlights illuminated the trees that lined the path, the leafless branches looming eerily out of the dark. "I'm sorry if I've got it wrong, Amy," he said at last. "It's just that I know how pressured I felt. All of my family expected that I'd go to med school, and in the end I wasn't sure whose dream it actually was."

"Until today," Amy said.

Matt nodded. "I know how families can mean the best but not always act like they do."

He pulled up in the brightly lit yard. Amy released her seat belt, Matt's words echoing through her mind. "I'm really happy that you know what you want now," she began.

"But?" Matt prompted. He switched the engine off and turned in his seat, his face half hidden by the shadows inside the car.

"No 'but,'" Amy said quickly. "I just wish that I could be as sure as you about my future."

"Maybe you need a crisis, too," Matt joked.

"Well," Amy said thoughtfully, "I'll keep that in mind, but I think I've got my hands full for now." Amy opened her door and then turned back toward Matt.

Matt looked at her, his eyes serious. "Amy, we'll all be proud of you, no matter what you do. So you should do what you really want."

Amy felt a shiver run up her spine as his words sank in. "I will," she promised.

Matt pulled the keys out of the ignition and pocketed them. "Now we get to deal with another episode in the wedding extravaganza," Matt mumbled.

Amy wasn't sure she was ready for whatever might be brewing in the house, either. As they climbed from the Jeep, the kitchen door opened and Lou stood in the yellow rectangle of light. Amy had phoned her from the hospital to let her know they were all safe and well. Lou held out her arms. "A good day's work," she said simply. "I'm very proud of you both."

Amy hugged her back, briefly resting her cheek on Lou's shoulder as fatigue dragged at her muscles.

They walked into the kitchen with Matt following, and Amy felt a rush of pleasure to see Joni, Ty, and Scott sitting around the table. "Three cheers for the heroes of the hour!" Scott pushed his chair back and raised his glass, grinning at Amy, who felt her cheeks begin to burn as the others cheered enthusiastically.

"Enough already," Matt laughed, crossing the room and giving Scott a brotherly punch on the shoulder.

Amy was content to be home and relieved that the mood was easy, with people she cared about gathered in the kitchen. Joni gave her a complete update on Tiger, mentioning that Scott had taken the blood samples and would have results within a couple of days. Joni also told her that Sundance was very brave heading back to Heartland through the wild gusts of snow. She made him a bran mash with chopped apples and carrots as a special treat.

Lou told Amy that Grandpa had stayed at Nancy's to avoid the bad roads and help her with snow removal in the morning.

Of course, there were many questions about Evan and the Holloways, too. Amy explained that it was luck that Sundance had jarred her memory about the new path. Everyone agreed it was fortunate that Evan had found a shelter in the woods, minimizing his exposure to the wind and snow. Once Amy got to the point where Matt and Joni had arrived, Matt took over the storytelling. As he recounted the harrowing rescue with a dramatic play-by-play, Amy found her mind drifting, replaying the conversation she and Matt had had in the car.

A few minutes later, the phone startled Amy from her thoughts. Lou rushed to pick it up in her office, and Amy looked around the table.

Ty leaned toward her. "Hey," he whispered in her ear. "I'm going to take off now. I'm going to drop Joni off since she doesn't have chains on her tires. I managed to get all the extra feed and sand we wanted, so we should be OK if the weather gets any worse."

Amy smiled gratefully. "Thanks, Ty. I'll see you tomorrow." Ty brushed the hair off her face and gave her a warm kiss. Amy thought forward to the morning, when Ty would arrive at the barn. She happily anticipated resuming their daily routine.

As Lou curled up with the phone in a chair in the corner of the room, Scott and Matt also pulled on their coats. "We're heading off, too, now that I have a ride home." Scott winked at Amy and turned to blow Lou a kiss. He looked at Matt. "Seriously, Matt, it sounds like you guys did really well today. Good work. This time, I'll let you off the hook for taking my car."

By the time Amy had closed the door behind Scott and Matt, she could hear her sister saying good-bye with a rather flat tone in her voice.

The moment her sister hung up the phone, Amy knew something was wrong. "That was Dad calling from the airport," she said. "Their connecting flight's been delayed because of the snow." She sighed and rested her head against the back of the chair, closing her eyes.

"But he'll still be here for the wedding, won't he?" Amy asked in alarm.

"It depends on the weather," Lou replied without opening her eyes. She began to massage her temples. "And so does putting up the tent, and the arrival of most of our guests, including Marnie, of course." Amy knew Lou's best friend was due to fly in from New York the next day.

Amy didn't know what to say. "It's only Wednesday, we've still got two whole days before Saturday," she pointed out, and then winced, realizing that was probably the worst thing she could have said.

"Two days," Lou echoed, her voice rising until it sounded on the edge of hysteria. "I don't want to get married without Dad and Helena here. It's bad enough that Mom won't be with me on my wedding day." She stood up and walked to the door, wiping her sleeve across her tear-stained face. Amy watched her, heartbroken.

"Don't worry, I just need a good night's sleep," Lou told her. "I think I'll go up and take a long bath."

Amy nodded, feeling it was probably best not to say anything else. As Lou left the room, Amy sank back down into a chair and rested her head on her arms. She understood Lou's disappointment. Her wedding would not feel as special if she couldn't share it with family and friends. Amy vowed to do whatever she could to make all the plans come together.

Suddenly, all of the day's events rushed upon her, and she felt a huge wave of exhaustion flood over her. The horses were all inside, cozy and warm, apart from Tiger, who was wearing so many blankets he could hardly stand. Lou's idea of a bath and an early night felt incredibly appealing, and there really was nothing else Amy could do to help anyone that day.

✌

Amy groggily opened her eyes the next morning and frowned at the daylight showing behind her curtains. "I slept through my alarm," she groaned, glancing at the time. She quickly threw back her duvet and grabbed her clothes, realizing she was already falling short on her plans to help Lou. Thinking about the weather, Amy pulled back the curtain and grinned at the sight of pale blue sky, sunlight warming the window. She looked down at the stable-block roof and saw that the snow on it was already melting. "Thank goodness," she whispered. With any luck, the clear skies would hold and Lou's wedding day could proceed according to plans.

Amy hurried straight to the office and found Lou on the computer. "Have you seen the weather?" she burst out.

Lou looked up and smiled, her expression a world away from the pale, anxious one from the night before. "Isn't it great?" she enthused. "I just phoned the tent company and they'll be here this afternoon. Scott and Matt are on their way to set up the heaters so the ground won't be too hard, and I've made up my mind that I want fresh flowers in my hair to match yours, instead of a tiara, and the florist said they'll take care of it." She hesitated, and the corners of her mouth turned down slightly. "I haven't heard from Dad, though."

Amy wanted to keep her sister upbeat. "Dad still might

make it. Don't give up on him yet," she insisted. "Everything else is falling into place, and since school is bound to be closed with all the snow, I'm all yours."

"Thanks, Amy. You could start by making some coffee and giving me the big mug." Lou smiled.

❧

Leaving her sister with a full mug, Amy carried a tray of steaming coffee across the snowy yard and into the barn, where Joni and Ty were finishing the last of the morning feeds. "Hey, Sleeping Beauty," Ty joked, leaving Belle's stall and bolting it behind him.

"Sorry." Amy smiled ruefully. "I was so beat, I didn't even hear the alarm."

"Don't worry, you needed the rest after yesterday," Ty told her as he took his coffee and stood beside her to look at the pretty black pony. "I'd like to try loading her again this afternoon," he said. "She walked halfway up the ramp yesterday morning. I think we might get her all the way in today. Placing a trail of alfalfa cubes up the ramp is a good trick, too. Her stomach is obviously stronger than her fear."

"That's great," Amy said in delight, watching the little pony nod her head up and down as she chewed her food. She placed her hand on Ty's arm. "I'm going to check on Magic now — I mean, Tiger. Do you want to come with me?"

"Sure."

While Amy walked down to the field with Ty, she listened to him describe how Tiger had trotted over the snow that morning when he had taken the pony his bucket of feed. "He held his tail way up, and he looked as if he were really enjoying the snow." Ty grinned.

He held the gate open for Amy before going over to the water trough. There he drew a hay net out of the water. He had left it there to soak so, if Tiger was allergic to dust as well as the other unknown trigger, they could rest assured that there would be no dust on the hay. Amy paused to watch the buckskin gelding, who had broken into a beautiful, high-stepping trot, snow flying from under each hoof and his breath forming clouds in the air. He skittered to a halt next to Ty, who rubbed his nose as he secured the dripping hay net to a post.

Amy suddenly had a pang of guilt that she hadn't yet told Ty about her idea of going to college. But she felt she couldn't tell him until she was certain, and it was moments like these that made the thought of leaving Heartland almost unbearable.

Amy and Ty climbed onto the gate and sat contentedly side by side, watching Tiger pull at the soaked hay. Amy didn't hear Scott until he was right behind them. "I come bearing news," he said, leaning against the fence.

"Don't do that!" Amy, jolted with surprise, nearly lost her balance on the gate. She pretended to be irritated but couldn't hide her excitement to hear Scott's update. "You have the test results already?"

Scott nodded, looking pleased. "You were right. He's not allergic to dust — although now that we know he has COPD, he needs to be kept away from anything that has the potential to clog his airways."

"So what did the results say he was allergic to?" Ty interrupted, jumping down from the gate.

"A chemical that can be found in creosote and some other paints and stains," Scott said.

"Creosote," Amy echoed. Her mind raced back to Jack touching up the barn doors and giving the stable block a fresh coat of paint. And hadn't Joni also mentioned using creosote as a wood preservative? Suddenly, everything fell into place. No matter how clean Joni had left that stall, it had still had the smell of the wood treatment. And since Jack had gone over the entire stable block, the aroma was intense. "I have to call the Holloways," she said. "Evan's going to be so excited when I tell him we've solved the mystery. He'll be happy to know his pony will be well again."

Amy rushed off, leaving Scott and Ty to follow more slowly. But when she reached the yard, everything was in chaos. A large white truck was parked, with its back doors wide open. Three men were passing long poles out from it. Jack's car was pulled up, and he and Nancy

were carefully walking up to the kitchen door, supporting Lou's wedding cake.

Amy hurried to help them but was stopped by the toot
of a car horn. She spun around to see a yellow taxi pull
up. Almost before it had stopped, the passenger door
opened.

Amy's heart leaped. "Dad!"

Chapter Eleven

Amy didn't know whom to go to first as the rear passenger door opened and Helena stepped out as well, holding Amy and Lou's half sister, Lily, in her arms. Tim strode deliberately across the yard and caught Amy in a huge hug.

"Let her go, Tim. The poor girl can't breathe." Helena sounded amused as Tim released Amy with a playful grin.

Amy hurried over to kiss Helena before smiling down at Lily. "Hello, Lily. You've grown!" she exclaimed, feeling a thrill at seeing the changes. When Amy had first met Lily she was just a toddler, but now she was a little girl. Lily stared at Amy for a while, sucking her thumb. Then she blinked her large brown eyes a couple of times and pulled her thumb out, announcing solemnly, "Amee."

"She remembers my name!" Amy looked at Helena, unable to hide a delighted smile.

"Of course she does," Helena laughed. "She looks at photos of you and Lou every day."

"You're here!" A thrilled voice carried over the yard. Lou rushed around the side of the house with a bag of tent pegs slung over her shoulder. "Oh, I'm so happy!" She hugged all of the family one by one and then stood back as Scott, Ty, Nancy, and Jack joined them for a round of introductions and handshakes.

Amy looked at her sister, who was surreptitiously wiping away tears, laughing and crying at the same time. Scott wrapped his arms around Lou and hugged her tightly. Amy slipped her hand into Ty's. "What a morning," she breathed, smiling up at him.

❢

"I still can't believe you made it," Lou remarked as Jack dished out bowls of casserole and passed them around the full kitchen table.

"The snow disappeared almost as quickly as it came," said Tim. "Which was just as well, considering I was about to hire a husky team if we didn't get out of that airport soon."

Everyone laughed, including Lily, who banged her plastic knife and fork on the table. Amy felt Ty put his arm around her shoulder and give it a quick squeeze. "You could have just called Amy. She's become an expert at cross-country in the snow," he joked.

"What?" Tim raised his eyebrows. "What sort of mad escapades have my daughter been up to now?"

Amy blushed. "Oh, it can wait," she said self-consciously.

"I'd like to hear this," Jack said, setting his fork down on the table. He had missed the drama of Evan's disappearance, and Lou deliberately had decided not to tell him in order to spare him the worry.

"It's a long story," Amy insisted, wanting the attention to return to Lou and the wedding.

"Story, story," Lily shouted from her place on Helena's knee.

"There, now we have to hear it. Lily insists." Helena smiled. "Unless you want to be blamed for a tantrum."

Amy realized that she had no choice, and as briefly as possible she described the events of the previous day, emphasizing Matt's contribution. "I called the Holloways just before lunch, and they said the nurses are having a hard time keeping him in bed." She smiled as she recalled the little boy's devotion to his pony and hoped they'd be reunited soon. However proud her family was of what she and Matt had done, it was impossible to describe how important rescuing Evan had been — for both of them.

❧

Later on, when Nancy and Helena were putting Lily to bed and Tim was helping Ty and Joni with the evening stable chores, Jack came into the living room to find Amy and Lou making last-minute seating arrangements.

Jack cleared his throat. "I've been waiting to get the two of you on your own." Amy and Lou stopped talking and turned to look at him. His expression was so solemn, Amy wondered what was on his mind as he sat on the opposite sofa. He looked at them both and placed an envelope on the coffee table. He hesitated for a moment, his eyes lingering on the envelope. Then he looked at his granddaughters.

"We haven't really said how much it would have meant to have Marion here for what would be one of the most important moments in her life," Jack began. He went on more strongly, "I've been incredibly proud of the way both you girls have shown such courage since your mom's death." Amy felt her eyes fill with tears as her grandpa pulled a handkerchief from his trouser pocket. He blew his nose before adding, "I just wanted to have a moment with you where we shared your mom together. She would have loved to be with you on your day, Lou."

Lou gripped Amy's hand as their grandpa picked up the envelope and pulled out an old black-and-white photo. Without saying another word, Jack passed it to them. It was a picture of their mom on her wedding day. Amy heard Lou's sharp intake of breath, and she knew why. Their mother was wearing a dress that was designed and detailed in almost exactly the same style as Lou's, right down to the open front panel revealing a lacy under-skirt. Lou ran her finger over the picture. Even the way Marion was wearing her hair was similar to the style Lou had finally decided on, with fresh flowers woven in and out of the loose blond ringlets.

Amy stared at the familiar face that looked so young and happy in the picture. "She's so beautiful," she whispered.

Jack nodded, and when Lou went to hand him back the photo, he held up his hands. "You keep it," he told her, standing up. "Just remember she will be there with you every step of the way tomorrow. You know she will."

Amy squeezed her sister's hand, knowing how much the photograph would mean to her. Lou glanced at her with a mixture of sadness and wistfulness and then she lifted her head and looked over Amy's shoulder. Amy twisted around and saw that her father was standing in the doorway, wiping his hands on a towel.

Jack nodded to Tim and stood up, heading for the stairs.

"I enjoyed helping out tonight," Tim said cheerfully, stepping into the room. "Your Spindleberry's a real char-acter. He reminds me of a youngster I bought last year."

Tim's eyes looked from Amy to Lou, and his lightheart-
edness faded. Tossing the towel over one shoulder, he
crossed the room to stand just behind the sofa. His gaze
fell on the photograph in Lou's hand. Lou instinctively
tried to cover it, but it was too late.

"May I see it?" Tim asked.

Wordlessly, Lou handed it to him. Amy felt her stomach twist as her father looked down at the picture, his
gray eyes serious. Tim brushed his finger gently over the
photograph before glancing up. "Wow. That's a nice
memory," he said. He swallowed and looked from Amy
to Lou. "Please don't ever feel that you have to hide
something like this from me," he said with a catch in his
throat.

"I remember when this was taken," he went on, smiling now. "Marion had tripped over her dress, and I had
only just managed to catch her. She laughed and
laughed. Your mom was always full of fun" — his voice
dropped — "and of hope and dreams. I see so much of
that in you. If I could give you one gift, Lou, it would be
that you and Scott could know the happiness that
we had, and share dreams the way we did." He narrowed his eyes and stared over their heads. "And I hope
that when the difficult times come, you won't run away
from your problems but will find your strength in each
other."

Amy felt her throat tighten. She pressed her lips

together, trying to fight the tears, but they still rushed down her cheeks. She reached up her hand to squeeze her dad's arm. Amy heard a sniffle from Lou as well, and her sister stood up and hugged their father. He ran his hand through her hair, and Lou smiled up at him. In an impulsive moment, Amy stood up, too, and she wrapped her arms around her family. She felt her father's arm on her back, and then, instead of a sob, she heard her sister's warm laugh.

❧

"Are you disappointed that your rehearsal dinner was canceled last night?" Helena paused to look questioningly at Lou.

"Not really. It was my fault for booking a restaurant out in the boonies," Lou told her. The snow had forced the restaurant to remain closed, and Lou hadn't been able to rebook anywhere at such short notice. "Besides, the minister was busy last night, so we couldn't have rehearsed anything anyway. It gives me more time to get everything done before tomorrow."

Helena nodded and returned her attention to the box from which she was counting the pouches of birdseed tied with ivory and lilac ribbon. She frowned, her hand hovering above the box.

Amy looked up from the shoes she was polishing. "Thirty-two."

"Thanks." Helena smiled, pushing her hair out of her eyes before plunging her hand back into the birdseed.

"Thank yooo," a small, high voice corrected her, and everyone laughed at Lily, who was toddling around the kitchen table, a wooden spoon clutched firmly in her fist.

"Careful," Helena called as Lily bumped into the table leg and sat down suddenly on her bottom.

"I'll take her outside," Nancy offered, getting up from her chair and holding out her hands to the toddler.

Lou finished signing the last check and then crossed through that line on her checklist, finishing by pushing her pencil behind her ear. "I'm going to have to run in a minute. I've got to pick up the capes before my appointment, since I couldn't run errands yesterday."

"Leave yourself plenty of time," Helena warned, putting the final tulle-wrapped birdseed ball on the table. "If you're rushed, you're sure to smudge your nails." Helena gave a teasing grin, not realizing that was a genuine concern of Lou's.

Lou had an appointment for a full facial and nail treatment at the salon in town. Helena let out an exaggerated sigh. "I'm just jealous. I wish I had an excuse to go with you." She looked across at Amy and gave her a wink.

"Well, why don't you come?" Lou offered. "It would be a lot more fun if you did — I tried to convince Amy, but she wasn't having any of it! Something about horses needing to be fed."

"Hey, manicured nails and horses don't go. All I can promise is that they'll be clean for tomorrow." Amy grinned, tucking her hands under her arms.

"Helena, as the bride, I insist you join me. There are enough people around to take care of Lily — that is, if anyone can steal her away from Nancy." Lou smiled and let out a deep breath. Even though she was still uptight about the wedding, there was an air of suppressed excitement about her. Her cheeks had a soft pink glow and her eyes were sparkling.

Amy decided to go outside as she buffed her shoes. It was lucky that a pair of Lou's heels matched the lilac dress perfectly. She sat on an upturned bucket and began to rub the soft leather. Ty smiled as he passed her, holding a grooming kit in one hand and trailer wraps in another. The snow was beginning to melt away, and the yard was already clear, with just the tiled stable-block roof still covered with a layer of snow. Amy listened to the steady drip of water falling from the gutters before she was distracted by the louder sound of a trailer pulling up.

She quickly stuffed the buffing cloth in the shoe and placed it on the deck. As she turned around, she saw Evan hurrying across the yard, his face stretched into a wide grin.

"We're here to get Tiger!" he called out, bounding

toward her like an overgrown puppy — an overgrown puppy in a hat, scarf, gloves, and fully zipped coat.

"He's all ready," Amy told him. She thought how different Evan looked from the last time she had seen him. His cheeks were rosy red, and his blue eyes darted around, taking in everything. Amy pointed to where Ty was putting wraps on Tiger, and Evan immediately skipped off.

"Ever since we left the hospital, it's been Tiger, Tiger, Tiger." Amy turned at the sound of Janet Holloway's voice and marveled at the change not just in Evan's face, but in hers, too. The last time Amy had seen Evan's foster parents, they had been consumed with worry. Now Janet looked years younger and she had a spring in her step, holding out her arms to clasp Amy in a warm hug.

"We can't thank you enough for everything you've done," she said, her voice full of emotion. Amy smiled at Chris over Janet's shoulder. He was almost invisible behind a giant potted fern that he was carrying in both hands.

"We're so glad we could help," Amy said when Janet finally let her go. She shrugged. "We were just in the right place at the right time, you know."

Chris carefully set down the potted plant. "We thought you might like to have this as a small token of our thanks."

"It's beautiful," Amy said, immediately picturing it in the entrance of the wedding tent or maybe on the altar. She placed her hand in Chris's outstretched one and tried to maintain an even smile as he squeezed hard, vigorously shaking it up and down. She couldn't help but feel relieved at the sound of hooves approaching — it gave her an excuse to take her hand back. Evan was leading Tiger, with Ty close behind. The little boy looked as if he was about to burst with pride as he patted the buckskin's neck.

"He looks great," Chris commented, not taking his eyes off them as Evan led Tiger up to the trailer. "We're glad he's better."

Amy left Chris and Janet and went over to join Evan by the trailer ramp. Amy rubbed the buckskin gelding on his cheek. "Good-bye, boy," she said in a low voice as he turned his head and lipped her coat sleeve. She knew Evan was watching her, and the last thing she wanted was for him to think she was sad that Tiger was leaving. She forced herself to smile and patted the gelding's neck, saying brightly to the young boy, "He's going to be fine now, but I hope to see you both back here in the spring."

Ty threw her a quizzical glance as he double-checked the buckles on Tiger's blanket.

"Evan and I are going to ride the cross-country trail," Amy told him.

"Ahh." Ty nodded, his expression serious. "Is it just the two of you, or is there an open invitation?"

"Oh, I think we might let you come, too. What do you think, Evan?"

"I guess," he said, a grin lighting up his freckled face.

"OK, then, first things first. Let's get this guy loaded," Amy said. She took hold of Tiger's halter as Evan clicked to the pony and began to walk up the ramp. Tiger didn't even hesitate. His hooves made a dull thudding sound against the wood as he walked steadily into the trailer.

Amy watched as Evan tied Tiger's lead rope. He seemed to be taking a long time with the knot, running the rope through his fingers over and over again. Without looking at her, he took a deep breath and said, "Janet and Chris want to adopt me."

Amy felt her heart skip. "That's wonderful," she said warmly.

Evan stretched his hand up to straighten Tiger's forelock. "Remember when you told me about that person you used to know? Who made you feel special?"

"I remember."

"It made me want to have someone like that." Evan spoke so quietly that Amy could hardly make out his words.

She reached out to give his shoulder a quick squeeze. "I'm really happy for you, Evan," she said. "Chris and

Janet seem like great people. And I'm sure they love you very much."

Evan nodded, keeping his gaze on Tiger, who stamped his foot restlessly.

"He wants to get home," Amy said. She paused to straighten the pony's blanket before following Evan out the side door. They helped Ty push up the ramp, and Amy secured the bolts automatically, her thoughts miles away as she considered Evan's words. She was thrilled that the boy had found people who loved him enough to step into the role of parents. It made her think of how so many people had gathered around to help and support her since her mom's death. Lou, Grandpa, Tim, Helena — even Nancy. Amy glanced sideways at Ty, who was securing the opposite bar. She loved the way his dark hair sometimes fell over one eye. He pushed it back and smiled at her. *And Ty*, she thought, feeling a rush of emotion. *No one could make me feel more special than he has.*

"All ready?" Chris's voice broke into her thoughts.

"Yep," Amy said, giving the ramp a tap.

Chris and Janet shook hands with Ty and Amy before climbing into their truck. Evan put one foot on the runner and hesitated. In one quick movement he turned and wrapped his arms around Amy's waist and gave her a swift, fierce hug. Startled, Amy returned his hug before Evan broke loose and swung himself up into the cab.

She swallowed hard as the trailer pulled slowly out of the yard. She'd grown incredibly fond of Evan over the past few days — Evan and Tiger. She hoped she would see them again.

"You OK?" Ty asked, slipping his arm around her waist and giving it a squeeze.

Amy nodded. "It's never easy seeing horses leave, but it's worth it to see them reunited with their owners."

"I agree. There's nothing like it," Ty agreed. "I guess it's what we do best."

🙢

Before getting into bed that night, Amy took one last look at the long, shimmery dress hanging on her closet door. She smoothed her hand down the cool silk and shook her head. She still couldn't quite face the fact that this was the last night she'd be sleeping under the same roof as her sister. Although she had tried, Amy simply couldn't imagine Lou not being there in the morning, scolding her for not having breakfast or teasing her for eating three whole servings of macaroni and cheese for dinner. Who would ask her about the boring details of her day? With whom would she laugh with over silly little things?

Amy looked at her dressing table, which was usually cluttered with horse magazines but now was covered with all of the things she would need for the next day —

a new pack of hose, underwear, makeup, shampoo, conditioner, and lots of bobby pins.

Amy pulled back her comforter and switched off her bedside light. *From this day on, everything will be different,* she thought, staring into the dark. She felt her stomach churn, and then it dawned on her. Even if Lou weren't getting married, the future still was not so certain. Lou might not be the only one who would be leaving Heartland.

Chapter Twelve

Amy opened her eyes at the sound of feet on the landing and the swish of the bathroom door opening and closing. It felt as if she had only been asleep for a few hours. She blinked, trying to gauge the time from the light coming in through her window. It was still dark. Amy groped about for her alarm clock before she remembered exactly what day it was. Her stomach jumped, and swung her feet purposefully off the bed. She had a million things to do before the wedding!

She pulled on a T-shirt, a thick wool sweater, and jeans before hurrying downstairs where someone had already put the kettle on to boil. Amy decided not to stop for coffee, and crossed the room to pull her winter coat off the peg. The moment she pulled open the door, she was hit by an icy wall of air. "Yikes!" she muttered, thinking of the dresses they would be wearing later. She reached up for her scarf and wrapped it around her neck before picking her way across the yard, careful not to slip on any lingering patches of ice.

Amy flicked on the barn lights and smiled to herself at the sight of horses' heads appearing, blinking their eyes against the sudden glare. "Morning, boys and girls," she said.

She went to the feed room and began to fill buckets with scoops of grain from the large silver bins. Her mind leaped forward to the day ahead, and her stomach whipped up a case of butterflies, a mix of nerves and excitement. It was still too early to figure out what the weather was going to do, but the temperature was definitely below freezing! Amy tucked her bright red scarf farther into her jacket before picking up several buckets and going back into the barn. When she passed the stall that Tiger had briefly been in, Amy smiled. If she were asked, she would bet that Evan was already up with his pony, grooming him and telling him about the cross-country trail for the hundredth time.

After she had distributed the buckets, she collected a grooming kit and made her way to Spindle's stall. Lou had planned to have some photos taken by the far pasture, and Amy thought it might be nice to have one of the horses grazing in the background to add to the atmosphere. "We've got to make you beautiful," she told the gelding, who ignored her pampering, his nose thrust deep inside his bucket.

She unbuckled Spindle's blanket and folded it back before removing it and placing it over the stall wall. She spent the next fifteen minutes smoothing his coat with a body brush and combing his mane and tail until the black hair ran through her fingers in a soft, silky curtain. "You clean up well," she told him as she gave his muzzle a kiss. Spindle blinked his dark brown eyes at her before resting his forehead against her chest. Amy smiled and reached up to scratch under his mane.

"Hey!" Joni's voice sounded behind them. Amy turned, startled. She hadn't heard the stable girl arrive. "I should have known you wouldn't be able to stay away!" Joni put her hands on her hips and pretended to look stern. "You have a wedding to get ready for, Ms. Maid of Honor. Come on now, out of there!"

Amy laughed and gave Spindle a quick pat before heading through the stall door, which Joni closed behind her. "Can you put his blanket back on for me? Oh, and I haven't collected any of the buckets yet, and . . ."

"Go!" Joni flapped her hands at Amy. "I think I can figure out what to do."

She shooed Amy all the way down the aisle and onto the yard before going back to the barn. It was light now, and Amy could see her breath forming clouds in the cold air. "Please don't let it snow," she muttered as she made her way across to Ty's car. He had pulled up right out-side the back door to make room for all of the antici-pated guests.

"Morning," Ty said. He carefully lifted his suit, zipped into a long black garment bag, out from behind the driver's seat. "Shouldn't you be in the house getting ready? Like putting your hair in curlers?"

"Not you, too." Amy laughed. "I've already been thrown out of the barn by Joni!"

"That girl is good at her job," Ty admitted, and gave Amy a quick kiss on her lips. "Can you take this inside for me so I can change later?"

"Sure." Amy took the suit and his polished black shoes before heading into the house. For once she real-ized she was looking forward to a long soak in a bubble bath after being out in the cold early morning air.

❧

Amy passed Lou on the landing. Her sister was wrapped in a fluffy white robe, with her hair in a towel. "What's the weather like?" Lou asked anxiously.

"Well, apart from the three feet of snow that fell in the night, it looks like it's going to be a fine day," Amy said, straight-faced.

Lou's eyes widened in disbelief before she realized that Amy was joking. "Don't do that to me!" She lightly punched her arm.

"Sorry," Amy grinned. "Couldn't resist."

"Try." Lou made a face at her before smiling back. "And while you're at it, get that hay out of your hair."

"Yes, ma'am!" Amy made a mock salute and hurried to her bedroom to get undressed.

✌

When Amy finally made her way back downstairs, it seemed as if a house party was going on. Her dad and grandpa were chatting in the living room, cups of coffee in their hands. They both turned an identical pained expression toward Amy as she walked through the room on her way to the kitchen. "Don't go in there," Tim joked, stretching out one hand as if to save her.

"It's worse than a war zone," Jack agreed.

"Cowards." Amy grinned until she walked into the kitchen and realized what they meant. Helena was feeding Lily her breakfast at one end of the kitchen table, the rest of which was completely filled with brushes, mirrors, and makeup. Nancy was cooking scrambled eggs at the stove, and the smell of autumn casseroles for the reception buffet came from the oven. The makeup artist had arrived and was rubbing cream into Lou's face. Suddenly, Amy realized who was sitting opposite Lou.

"Marnie!"

The attractive blond girl turned in Amy's direction

and pushed her chair away from the table. "Hey, Amy." Her face broke into a wide smile.

Amy hurried across the room to hug her, dodging a carry-on bag and a garment bag on the way. "We were beginning to think you wouldn't be able to make it with all the airport delays."

"Are you kidding? I camped out in the terminal and refused to leave. The first flight out of there had my name on it."

Amy pulled up a chair and poured herself a coffee. Lou had her eyes closed and her head tipped back, and as Amy studied her sister's delicate face, she felt a flood of affection for her. It was Lou's wedding day. The mere idea filled Amy with awe. Her sister was the bride, practically a celebrity!

Lou half opened her eyes and mumbled without moving her lips, "Amy, tie back your hair." She tapped her hand down on the tabletop where there was a pile of rubber bands and barrettes. Amy obediently secured her hair away from her face and then put back her own head for the beautician to begin rubbing the moisturizing cream into her skin.

When she was finally allowed to look into a mirror, she blinked in surprise. She rarely wore makeup and was amazed at how different she looked. Her gray eyes, lined with dark pencil, looked much larger than usual, and her face was more angular, her cheekbones accentuated by with the rose-tinted blush. She pressed her lips together, the gloss feeling slick and slightly uncomfortable. But Amy was pleased with the makeup, even if it felt odd. She didn't think her face looked over-done; she had dreaded the possibility of electric-blue eyeshadow and bright pink lipstick.

The back door banged open, followed by a blast of cool air, and Soraya.

"Wow! You all look gorgeous." Soraya stared at the three of them, her eyes wide. She was holding her dress in a plastic cover, draped over her arm. "I thought I'd get changed here, if that's all right?"

Amy smiled. "I'm glad you came. We can all help each other get dressed. My bridesmaid dress has this annoy-ing clasp."

"Hey, none of that!" Lou insisted, only somewhat in jest. Marnie giggled.

"What's the weather like?" Lou asked Soraya, a note of anxiety in her voice as she stood up and crossed to the window.

"It's cold, but it's turning out to be really nice. Lots of sun," Soraya said reassuringly. "And I peeked inside the tent on the way in — it looks wonderful, Lou!"

"Are all the chairs out?" Lou lifted her hand to run it through her hair like she always did when she was ner-vous, but then realized it was styled stiff with hairspray.

"Hey, take deep breaths and drink some more coffee,"

Marnie interjected as Nancy set down a fresh pot on the table.

"Don't you mean less?" Helena laughed, balancing Lily on her hip as she collected the dirty cups from the table. "I have some chamomile tea if anyone wants it. It's very calming."

"I just passed your dad and grandpa on their way out to supervise everything," Soraya told Lou. "All of the chairs are out, and the twinkle lights are in place. I saw someone taking a stack of white tablecloths out of a truck. From what I could tell, everything's under control."

Amy smiled gratefully at her best friend. She had said exactly the right thing to keep Lou from working herself into a panicked frenzy. As long as they could all keep the bride calm, everything would be fine!

❧

Soraya helped to ease the dress over Amy's head so that her hair wouldn't get ruined and her makeup wouldn't be smudged. Soraya pulled up the zipper and took a step back. "You look absolutely stunning," she declared. "Ty won't be able to keep his eyes off you."

Amy smoothed the lilac silk. "I don't know how much anyone will see of this dress. I plan to have that cape on all night. It's too cold to wear anything but jeans and long underwear." She grimaced, rubbing her hands together.

"Well, it's warmer than the day before yesterday, and you were willing to be outside then," Soraya said, sitting down on the edge of the bed. "Matt told me all about what happened. Life's just one drama after another for you! A rescue two days ago, now a wedding."

Amy smiled and then put her hand to her mouth, remembering her friend's audition. "Speaking of drama, did you hear?" Otterbein College was supposed to notify Soraya if she had been accepted by their drama program.

"Yeah, I heard," Soraya said with a huge sigh.

When she heard Soraya's deflated tone, Amy regretted asking. Then a huge smile lit up Soraya's face, and she jumped up on the bed. "I got in, I got in, I got in!" she yelled, spinning around and laughing.

Amy burst out laughing as well. "That's the best news ever!" Amy exclaimed. Soraya leaped to the floor and hugged her.

"I know. I think Otterbein is my first choice. I'm just so glad that's over," Soraya admitted.

Hearing those words, Amy knew how relieved Soraya must have felt. She wondered if she should tell Soraya about her own hopes and goals, but she knew it wasn't the right time. This moment was Soraya's, and she had earned it.

❧

Amy stood at the bottom of the stairs with her father, grandpa, Marnie, and Lou. Her teeth were chattering from the cold and nerves. But when she looked up at her sister's face, she was struck by how composed she looked.

Lou took a deep breath. "This is it." She picked up her bouquet of white roses intertwined with trailing ivy. Amy faced Lou and smoothed out her fur-lined cape once more before stepping back to admire her. Everything was perfect, from the fresh flowers laced through Lou's golden ringlets to the delicate ivory satin shoes on her feet.

The front door was open, and they could hear music from the string quartet, drifting across the lawn. "You look beautiful," Tim told Lou in a husky voice. Lou slipped her hand onto his arm and squeezed it gently. She then held out her other hand to Jack, who patted it wordlessly, his smile telling Lou all she needed to know.

"Let's go," Lou said. "Marnie, you're first."

Marnie smiled and walked out the door, holding her bouquet. When she reached the bottom of the stairs, Amy started walking. As they crossed the garden, Amy couldn't help but feel as if she were in the middle of a dream. She could see the audience of friends and family illuminated by pale sunlight where they sat inside the tent, the flaps tied back with bows of tulle. Marnie and Amy walked down the aisle and took their places at the front. Amy gave Matt, the best man, a smile before she turned toward the guests.

As the familiar chords of the stringed instruments filled the tent, everyone rose to their feet. Lou was halfway down the aisle when she came into Amy's view. Even though Amy had seen her sister just moments before, she still caught her breath at the sight of her, decked out in her bridal gown. With Jack and Tim on either side, Lou was glowing with joy. They made their way between the seats and stopped in front of the ivy-covered trellis where Scott was waiting.

Amy was so happy for her sister that the minister's address washed over her. She surveyed all the smiling faces in the audience, and her eyes stopped on one.

Ty seemed intent on the minister, but then he glanced over at Amy. His expression didn't change, but he looked deep into her eyes. Amy was caught in his gaze. She thought how handsome he looked in his suit — different from the Ty on the yard, yet just as familiar. She couldn't help but smile at him. That's when Amy heard Lou and Scott speak the fateful words, "I do."

The next thing she knew, Lou and Scott were exchanging rings, kissing, and walking happily down the aisle. After all the preparation, they were now husband and wife. And now it was time to celebrate.

✼

Amy sat next to Matt in the tent, surrounded by twinkling lights. As they sipped their champagne, Amy leaned back in her chair, sighing with contentment. "If I eat a single thing more, I'm going to burst out of this dress," she said, adjusting her waistline.

"You wouldn't want to upstage the bride like that," Matt joked.

Amy shook her head at him and then realized that the music had changed from classical selections of the quartet to the opening chords of a love song. She looked around the room and saw Scott hold out his arm to escort Lou from the table to the dance floor. Amy noticed that her father and Helena and Nancy and Jack all had stopped chatting to watch the couple's first dance. Even Lily, in her pretty rose-colored dress, seemed mesmerized.

Lou rested her head on Scott's shoulder as they began to move to the music. Scott was incredibly handsome in his tuxedo, and as cameras began to flash, Amy thought that they looked as if they had stepped out of the pages of a magazine.

"I think as best man and maid of honor, we're supposed to dance the second dance together," Matt said, standing up and offering her his hand. He looked at Ty, who was sitting on the other side of Amy. "Do you mind if I steal your girl?"

Ty gave a shrug. "That depends. Would you mind me doing the same?" He gave Soraya a playful smile.

Soraya put her hands on her hips. "You guys know we can dance with whomever we want, don't you? Ty, you don't have to ask permission to dance with me."

Amy knew the dialogue was meant in jest, but she found herself wishing she weren't obligated to share her first dance with Matt. She suddenly wanted to be alone with Ty. But with her hand in his, Amy followed Matt to the dance floor.

They fell silent for a while, and Amy looked around the tent as they swayed to the music. Hundreds of tiny silver lights interwoven with ivy around the pillars gave the tent a fairy-tale atmosphere. Each table held a lamp that spilled soft light onto the beautiful ivory cloths. Everywhere Amy looked, people were chatting and smiling.

"Have you thought any more about your plans for the future?" Matt's question pulled Amy back to reality.

She took a deep breath because, as she had watched her sister take an important step in her life, she realized she was ready to take one of her own, too. Working with Tiger, Amy had realized that her instinct and devotion would get her only so far in her dedication to Heartland. She often wished she could do more, and veterinary training would make that possible. "Yes," Amy said slowly, deliberately. "I'm going to apply for the pre-veterinary program at Virginia Tech."

Matt's eyes lit up and his arms tightened around her waist. "Amy, that's fantastic! You'll get in. I'm sure of it. And I know you're going to love it. You'll make a great vet."

Amy was glad for his support at that moment. They had shared so much recently, and now it looked as if they were mapping out similar futures, too. But for all Matt's excitement, Amy felt almost solemn about her decision.

"Hey, guys. Looking at you, no one would ever guess this was a happy occasion." Amy glanced up and saw Ty was standing next to them, his hand resting on Soraya's shoulder. Amy realized that the next song had started playing.

"Oh, we were just talking," Matt said, releasing Amy from his arms and holding his hand out to Soraya. "But now we've all got dancing to do."

Ty slipped his arms around Amy's waist and pulled her close. "Did I tell you how beautiful you look?" he whispered.

Amy nodded and leaned her head against his shoulder.

"Good, I'm glad I told you," he said.

"You don't look so bad yourself," she murmured, resting her hand on his shoulder.

"It's been a great day," Ty said. "You guys were great. Everything went as planned."

"Except when Spindle decided to eat the flowers in

Lou's hair," Amy reminded him. Amy smiled as she remembered how the colt had disrupted a photo op by sampling the bride's hair accessories.

"So how are you feeling, now that it's just going to be you and your grandpa at home?" Ty asked. As always, his question got right to the heart of the matter.

Amy's hand grasped Ty's shoulder a little tighter. She knew she couldn't put off telling him about her decision to apply to college much longer, but she couldn't bring herself to spoil this wonderful day. "I still have you," she answered, running her fingers along his jacket's seam.

"You'll always have me."

Ty's arms tightened around her, and he began to hum along with the music. Lou passed them. The bride held Lily in her arms, the little girl playing with one of her ringlets. They were followed closely by Helena and Tim, holding hands and looking as happy as the newlyweds. Amy's heart was warmed by the thought that everyone important in her life was here to share her sister's joy.

With her hands still on his shoulders, Amy stood back and gazed into Ty's kind green eyes. A real ache began to grow inside with the thought that she was about to change everything.

But for now things could be perfect. On another day, she would tell Ty that she was leaving Heartland.

Come home to Heartland one last time...

In this moving conclusion to the beloved series, Amy is graduating from high school. She knows she should feel excited for college, but she dreads leaving home. And now she must decide what her future holds, and whether it will take place at—or away—from Heartland.

www.scholastic.com/titles/heartland

Discover the place where neglected horses learn to trust again.

Visit Heartland

on the Web
scholastic.com/heartland

- Join Amy and share her adventures
- Read sample chapters from the Heartland books
- Collect the new Heartland trading cards
- Find out about Heartland writing contests and much more